Romeo Falls

Amy Briant

Bella
BOOKS

2012

Bella Books, Inc.
P.O. Box 10543
Tallahassee, FL 32302

Printed in the United States of America on acid-free paper
First published 2012

Cover Designer: Sandy Knowles

ISBN 13: 978-1-59493-267-0

PUBLISHER'S NOTE

Other Bella Books By Amy Briant

Shadow Point

For lonely hearts.

And Volkswagen enthusiasts.

About The Author

Amy Briant's first book, *Shadow Point*, won a Goldie for Best Debut Author as well as an Alice B. Lavender award for lesbian fiction debut novel. She lives in the San Francisco Bay Area. Find out more at www.amybriant.com.

PROLOGUE

A thousand stars twinkled in the midnight blue midwestern summer sky, their reflections in the lake below like diamonds tossed carelessly across velvet. In the distance, the women's music festival crowd screamed and cheered for the headlining band, but all was serene and quiet on the cool sandy shore of the lake. Ten feet from the water's edge, a leather carpenter's belt with a hammer in it sat atop a loose pile of clothes. Other clothes were randomly strewn about. A half-empty wine bottle reposed in a much used yellow suede work boot. Strategically placed citronella candles kept the mosquitoes at bay. In the center of their gentle glow, a young woman sat on a blanket. Twenty-six-year-old Dorsey Larue peered into the darkness, straining to see the girl with whom she had just made love.

A muted splash caught her attention. Another splash followed, then the dim figure of a nude woman emerged from the shadows of the lake.

And what a figure, thought Dorsey, deeply inhaling the warm night air. The anonymous girl's quiet charm, coupled with the sardonic, intelligent gleam of her piercing blue eyes behind stylish glasses had first attracted Dorsey. The discovery of the lush, soft curves augmenting the slender form beneath the tattered jeans and festival tank top had been like unwrapping an unexpected and wonderful gift.

Drops of water, silver in the moonlight, slowly and sinuously snaked their way down the girl's naked body as she strode, unhurried but sure of foot, back to their blanket. She had a distinctive heel-to-toe gait, slow but oh so confident. She looked more like a goddess than a girl in the luminous glow of the moon and stars, Dorsey thought—a Naked Silver Lake Goddess.

She found herself holding her breath as the other woman gracefully sat down next to her on the blanket. Dorsey reached for her favorite old flannel shirt, the one with the sleeves cut off, to dry off her companion.

"You're wet!" she exclaimed. An obvious, even fatuous thing to say, she knew, but what else do you say to a dripping wet naked girl? Even if you're naked too. She dabbed the flannel against the smooth fair skin of the girl's back, trying her best not to seem rushed or clumsy, though her heart was going a hundred miles an hour. The Goddess smiled at her over her pale shoulder, then raised her strong slender arms to run her hands through her dripping short black hair. When she shook it out, though, she only showered the both of them with a cascade of mercurial droplets. Laughing, they wrestled playfully for a moment, then lay panting together, entwined on the soft fleece blanket.

"Now we're both wet," the girl said in her low, throaty voice, with a secret little smile that made Dorsey's heart jump in a manner both alarming and exciting. The Goddess's fingertips traced a path down the taller girl's well-defined stomach. Their lips met for a kiss still tingling with the passion of their first embrace. As Dorsey's hands slid down to the girl's hips to pull her in tighter, she heard the far-off singer say, "Thank you! Good night!" The crowd roared one last time, then the sound faded to a dull, happy rumble as they started packing up to leave, the concert over.

The Goddess's hand was between Dorsey's legs now, her fingers seeking and finding a particular spot they had so recently learned.

"Oh, God," said Dorsey. "Oh, *God*..."

"Oh, God," said the Goddess, but in a completely different tone of voice. She suddenly stopped what she was doing and sat up. Listening intently, she said, "Do you hear anything?"

"What? What's wrong?" a bewildered and unsatisfied Dorsey asked, reaching for the other girl's hand. Anything to get that hand back where it belonged.

But the Goddess sprang to her feet, scrambling for her scattered clothes. She pulled on her tattered jeans at high speed, saying, "Shit! I'm going to miss my ride!"

As a stunned and open-mouthed Dorsey watched, the girl crammed her feet into sneakers, grabbed a shirt off the ground (Dorsey's, as it turned out) and sped off topless toward the tree-lined forest path leading back to the festival.

"Sorry!" she called over her shoulder.

"Wait!" Dorsey cried as she disappeared from sight. "What's your name?"

But the Goddess was gone, into the night.

CHAPTER ONE

The bell rang cheerfully as a customer came in the front door of Larue's Swingtime Hardware. It was a typical Saturday afternoon at the store with Benny Goodman playing quietly in the background. The cats were asleep in the front display window, each in his jealously guarded spot in the dappled May sunshine. Dorsey glanced up from behind the cash register to see the round, beaming face of her best friend, Maggie. Since Dorsey was ringing up a sale, Maggie gave her a wave, picked up a basket and headed down aisle six, the first aisle by the door—paint, brushes, ladders and tarps.

"Thanks again, ladies," Dorsey said with a smile, handing over the bag containing a fancy coffeemaker to Mrs. Alene White, who nodded curtly but failed to return the smile. Mrs. White's pouty teenaged daughter Jimalene sighed gustily, saying,

"Come *on*, Mother! I was supposed to meet my friends at the pool fifteen minutes ago."

Dorsey kept the polite smile in place as the mother and daughter, now bickering, went out the door, then went in search of Maggie. She was still in aisle six, studying the locked cabinet in which the spray paint was displayed.

"Need some paint, Mags?"

"Oh, hey!" Maggie's face lit up in a smile. Enthusiastic and outgoing by nature, she was extra happy about something that day, Dorsey could tell.

Although the same age, the two lifelong friends were otherwise a study in contrasts. Maggie was five foot three, a little on the plump side, with pink cheeks, lively brown eyes and long dark hair pulled back conservatively in a twist. Also straight, divorced for a year now from Dwayne Bergstrom (thank God!) and the math teacher at the high school, a job she absolutely loved although it didn't require many of the skills she'd learned while acquiring her MBA.

Dorsey, on the other hand, was tall and lean at five foot eight. Her blond buzz cut had grown shaggy since early spring and was currently sticking out every which way due to a generous application of hair gel that morning. She knew she should get it cut again, but it was too much of a hassle. Especially since her choices were the barber shop, where they would give her shit, or the Kut, Kolor 'N' Kurl where they would give her more. The last time, she'd made her younger brother Shaw do it with some clippers at home. That did not go particularly well as Shaw was (a) easily distracted and (b) not a slave to symmetry.

The contrast continued into the two women's wardrobes. Dorsey had chosen comfort over style that morning (and every other morning) with dark blue Dickies work pants, ancient black engineer boots and a "Grover City Schwinn" T-shirt. One thing about working for the family business, at least she got to wear whatever she wanted. Maggie, as always, was perfectly turned out and color coordinated in a cantaloupe-colored capri pant ensemble. Fancy white sandals with a little heel, a slender white belt with gold accents, a white leather purse and lots of gold jewelry completed the look. Lots of makeup for Maggie, zero for Dorsey. Despite their many differences, or maybe because of them, the two had been fast friends since their first day of kindergarten at Romeo Falls Elementary when Maggie stood up for the little blond girl the other kids were already calling "tomboy" and Dorsey kicked Dwayne Bergstrom's butt for throwing sand in Maggie's face.

"So what's the paint for? And what color?" Dorsey asked her buddy, unlocking the cabinet.

"Oh, um, red and we're thinking about repainting those old Adirondack chairs on the porch, but that's not what I came down to tell you. You'll never guess who showed up last night!"

Maggie's eyes were dancing with excitement. Someone had shown up? Meaning he or she had voluntarily come to the tiny town of Romeo Falls of their own free will? Maggie was right— Dorsey couldn't begin to imagine who that could be.

"Well, who?" she asked, automatically selecting the best type of spray paint for the job and handing Maggie some cans which she put in her basket.

"Sarah!" Maggie said with delight.

"Your cousin? From the city?"

"Yes!" Maggie was obviously thrilled to pieces that her older cousin Sarah had come for a visit. Dorsey wasn't sure she shared her enthusiasm, but tried to appear positive for Maggie's sake.

"Wow," she said, not really meaning it as she relocked the cabinet.

"I know," Maggie gushed happily. "I can't believe you two finally get to meet!"

For their annual visit, Maggie's family had always gone to the cousins in the city (leaving Dorsey bereft for those two weeks each summer) and never the other way around. Dorsey had always felt a little jealous, honestly, of the girl she'd never met but heard so much about. Throughout her childhood, a series of framed school pictures of Sarah on Maggie's dresser showed a gawky, skinny girl with braces and truly unfortunate oversized plastic spectacles with tinted lenses and frames in "fashion" colors. Dorsey didn't see what the big deal was. But Maggie, with no siblings of her own, had looked up to Sarah, who was four years older, with all the extravagant infatuation of a young girl.

She was convinced that her big city cousin was everything she, Mary Margaret Bigelow, was not—thin, cultured, sophisticated and mature.

"So, where is this famous cousin of yours?" Dorsey said, hoping that hadn't come out too sarcastic. If it had, Maggie gave no sign. She turned toward the front window to peer out onto Main Street.

"She's parking her car—I made her let me out first because I was so excited to tell you! And, oh my gosh, you should see her adorable little car, Dorse! It's a *V-W*."

She whispered the letters as if they were something naughty. And maybe they were. People bought American in Romeo Falls. Dorsey shaded her eyes against the afternoon sun and glanced out the front window. Sure enough, a bright red Bug was sliding into a spot in front of the bank a block away. A little too cutesy, Dorsey thought, then told herself she was being childish.

Maggie bubbled on. "She's not sure how long she'll stay, but it might be for the whole summer! Isn't that fantastic?"

No, Dorsey thought mulishly, but nodding and smiling neutrally for Maggie's benefit. Not fantastic at all. She realized it was a little silly at twenty-six to be experiencing the emotions of a six-year-old, but darn it, she was not looking forward to sharing her one and only best friend's attention with a stranger this summer. Her life in Romeo Falls was bleak enough already— without Maggie, she'd be lost. Maggie's college years had been torture for Dorsey. She was so glad to have her best friend back now, even if it seemed like a waste for an MBA to be teaching math to a bunch of teenagers. In this town, for the most part, the only number they cared about was the 4 in 4-H. But Maggie enjoyed teaching.

The short list of things that currently brought joy to Dorsey's life included her friendship with Maggie, swimming at the community center pool and her hobby of restoring vintage furniture. She guessed she should include her job and her family, which were basically one and the same. And that was basically it for the List of Good Things. Her occasional freelance carpentry jobs brought in a little extra money, but let's face it, she sighed— she was stuck in Romeo Falls. Stuck in a dead-end job, stuck living in the same house with her brothers where they'd all three grown up, stuck in a boring life with absolutely zero romance. Just... stuck.

Further conversation was put on hold as another customer came through the door. Old Mr. Gustafson, an elderly but still hale and hearty farmer was in the market for a new hacksaw. A steady trickle of shoppers was the norm on Saturdays. The hardware store did a pretty good business, being the only establishment of its kind in town. But a recently opened "big box" home center store in the nearest metropolis—Grover City with some fifteen thousand souls sixty miles to the east—was her older brother Goodman's latest headache. He'd already noticed a trend of Romeo Falls residents buying their big ticket power tool purchases in Grover instead of at Larue's Swingtime Hardware. Short of slashing his prices to the point where he'd take a loss, he had not yet figured out a solution.

Having accepted the economic realities of her hometown at a young age, Dorsey was a reluctant but resigned employee of the family business. What else could she do? She certainly wasn't a farmer. College hadn't beckoned as she wasn't much of a student either. And she couldn't imagine working at the supermarket or the Sizzle'N'Shake. The hardware store, although far from her dream job, was at least comfortable and familiar. It was home, maybe even more so than the house.

The bell jangled again as she finished up with old Mr. Gustafson at the register. He was blocking her view of the front door, but hearing Maggie greet the newcomer, she assumed it was the cousin. Sarah. Their voices moved off down the paint aisle.

With a twinkle in his eye, Mr. Gustafson said in a tone of kindly reproach, "Such a pretty girl like you should be wearing a dress, Dorsey Lee."

She knew the old man, who had been a friend of her grandfather's, meant no offense. He told her she should be wearing a dress almost every time he saw her, despite the fact that the last time she'd worn one was in the third grade. The kids who had teased her so unmercifully in kindergarten for being a tomboy had teased her even more when she wore a dress, she'd found. And then moved on to tape "lezzy" signs to her high school locker. Their homophobia was less overt these days, but it was still no fun being the town pariah. But what else was new? She'd always been an outsider in Romeo Falls.

"Maybe next time, Mr. Gustafson," she told him with a smile, her standard reply. She thanked him for his purchase and shook his hand. Small-town business was all about the relationships, Goodman was always telling her and Shaw. So she smiled and smiled, asked about their families and thanked them for their business.

With not too bitter a heart, she hoped.

Maggie and her mystery companion were still lost in the depths of aisle six. The bell jangled as Mr. Gustafson departed, then Maggie called out, "Hey, Dorse? Can you help us out with this paint? I think we might want some blue too, maybe."

"Sure," Dorsey called back. She walked toward the front door and turned the corner into Paint.

Where she froze, her heart in her throat and all the air suddenly gone from her lungs. For there—in aisle six of Larue's Swingtime Hardware, holding a can of red spray paint and talking with Dorsey's best friend—was the Naked Silver Lake Goddess.

CHAPTER TWO

Not naked, of course. In fact, she was attractively attired in a well-worn, close-fitting pair of jeans, black V-neck T-shirt and a stylish hip length black leather jacket of supple lambskin. It had been a cool spring thus far, but the summer heat was just around the corner according to the *Farmer's Almanac*. And the Weather Channel. Seeing Sarah's casual but chic outfit, Dorsey was suddenly keenly aware of her own fashion choices, or lack thereof. Oh, well. Nothing she could do about it now.

Maggie came forward, looking perplexed at Dorsey's pole-axed reaction.

"Come on," she said, laughing and grabbing her best friend's arm to snap her out of her trance. "I want you two to finally meet."

As she performed the introductions, Dorsey stole another

look at Sarah's face. Yep, no doubt about it—she was definitely
the girl from that night by the lake last summer. Their meeting
had been all too short, but certainly memorable. Every moment
of it, in fact, was etched in Dorsey's brain.

"Nice to meet you," Dorsey said, briefly clasping Sarah's
cool hand.

"Likewise," was the reply.

The city girl's smile was cool and impersonal too. She
gave no sign that she recognized Dorsey who felt a hot flush
of embarrassment and chagrin starting at the base of her neck.
Should she say something? Or just forget about it—Sarah
obviously had. And to think of all the times Dorsey had dreamed
of the Goddess since that night. She had replayed their time
together over and over in her mind. Thought of her touch, of
touching her. Of what might have been...

Things clearly were not going the way Maggie had envisioned.
Puzzled by their stilted exchange, she said to them, "Well, you
two chat for a moment, okay? I'm just going to run to the little
girls' room."

Setting her basket down, she hurried off to the tiny restroom
by the office in the back of the store. Dorsey's brother had
declared it off limits to customers, but Maggie was practically
family. And besides, Good wasn't there at the moment. The
silence was getting awkward, Dorsey felt. Say something! she
ordered herself. And of course could not think of a single thing
to say. Sarah still held a can of spray paint in her hand. Her
slender, pale fingers wore no rings, Dorsey noticed.

"Did you have a question about the paint?" Dorsey finally
asked her, deciding on the professional approach. She could play
it cool too and hide behind the facade of customer service.

Sarah glanced blankly at the can in her hand. Her dorky
spectacles were long gone, along with the gawky child she no
longer resembled. She now wore a small fashionable pair of
thin black frames with clear rectangular lenses. Cute, Dorsey
thought, then caught herself. Don't go there, she warned
herself—she doesn't even remember you. But she couldn't keep
from automatically registering a few aspects of the other woman's
appearance—the same things she'd found so compelling at the

festival: the cute glasses, that promising gleam in the eye, the soft black hair in a delicately spiky cut and the deceptively slim body beneath the jeans and jacket. Not the type of face you'd see on a magazine cover, maybe, but an attractive, intelligent face nonetheless. A nice face.

My type of face, Dorsey thought with an inner sigh. And what a body...

Sarah's eyes met hers for a moment, then flicked back to the can of paint in her hand.

"Oh, yeah, the paint," she said, her voice low and a little husky, just like Dorsey had remembered it. She felt the tiniest jolt in her stomach at the alluring sound of that voice. Sarah hesitated, darting a glance over Dorsey's shoulder where Maggie had gone. "Oh, hell," she said suddenly and decisively, startling Dorsey.

"What?"

"Are we alone?" Sarah asked in an undertone.

"Well, yeah, until Maggie comes back."

"Look," Sarah said, then paused, staring deep into Dorsey's eyes, seemingly trying to gauge her reaction. She then went on in a rush, her words tumbling out. "I'm sorry. I owe you an apology. And a shirt too, I guess."

Dorsey felt a warm rush deep in the heart of her. *She remembers! She remembers!* She couldn't help but smile at Sarah, eliciting a small smile back.

"I still have yours," Dorsey told her. Not adding that she'd been sleeping in the soft festival tank top ever since that night. Sleeping... and dreaming.

"Look," Sarah said again, speaking rapidly and urgently while taking a step closer. To Dorsey's delight, she reached out to touch her bare arm. "I'm really sorry about that night and about just now, but I'm not out to Maggie or anyone else in the family here. Do you understand?"

Sarah's face was tilted up to look imploringly in Dorsey's eyes. The soft black leather of her coat brushed Dorsey's hip. Her hair smelled faintly of apples.

"Oh," was all Dorsey could say, finding herself dazzled by Sarah's sudden closeness, as well as somewhat nonplussed by her confession. Especially since Dorsey had been out to Maggie and everybody else since, well, since forever. And Maggie had always been the best friend a girl could ever wish for.

But everyone's situation was different. Dorsey understood that. Who knew what Sarah had been through, that forced her to keep her very identity secret and separate from her own family?

Maggie was bustling back down the aisle toward them, the grin on her face showing how thrilled she was to see them in close conversation. Sarah shot Dorsey a meaningful and entreating look, eyes wide behind her glasses, then took a step back.

"I get it," Dorsey said quietly to her in an undertone. "But... can we talk later?"

Sarah nodded gratefully. As Maggie rejoined them, Dorsey resumed the paint conversation, acting as if nothing of import had passed between her and Sarah, although she felt like a dog to be playacting in front of Maggie. The three of them walked slowly up to the cash register, chatting about nothing much.

"You'll come to brunch with Mother and us tomorrow, right?" Maggie said to Dorsey as she rang up the purchase. A meal with Mrs. Bigelow senior was not normally much of a draw for Dorsey. Sarah, who obviously knew her aunt well, took in Dorsey's reluctant expression with an arched eyebrow and a small smile.

Maggie said, "Come on, Dorse, I promise you Mother Bigelow will be on her best behavior. Especially with Sarah here."

Sarah suddenly grinned at Dorsey, which brought back that jolt in the stomach feeling and sealed the deal. Maybe with the three of them outnumbering the old bat, it would be a fair fight for once. Mrs. Bigelow disapproved of Dorsey's "lifestyle" (as the older woman put it), was a general pain in the ass and had done many subtle and not-so-subtle sly things over the years to try and break up the friendship between her daughter and Dorsey, or at least put some distance between them. All her efforts had been futile so far, but she hadn't given up yet. Vivian Bigelow was no quitter.

"All right," Dorsey acquiesced with a shrug and a grin. "Eleven o'clock at the café?"

"Right," Maggie said. "Right after church. Unless you want to join us?" She should have known from long experience that Dorsey's answer would always be no, but couldn't seem to stop herself from asking anyhow.

"I'll meet you at the restaurant," was Dorsey's reply. From Sarah's look, she would have preferred that too, but there was no way Mother Bigelow would let her skip church, not with Sarah staying under her roof. Maggie had moved back in with her parent after her divorce from Dwayne Bergstrom the past year. There were no apartments in Romeo Falls and without the money to buy a house of her own, her options were limited. She had been saving her money steadily, but was still a long way from a down payment. She'd been talking about renting a mobile home in the trailer park just to get out from under her mother's bossy thumb, but was too scared to break it to her, Dorsey thought. The old battle-ax would probably throw a fit when she heard.

Gathering up her purchases, Maggie said, "Well, we're off to Grover for dinner with Cousin Buell and his family. Since this is Sarah's first visit here, we're making the rounds. But we'll see you tomorrow, right, Dorse?"

Dorsey nodded, taking a seat on the stool behind the counter. To her surprise, Sarah then leaned across and took her hand.

"It was a real pleasure meeting you for the first time, Dorsey," she said, the pressure of her fingers and the laugh in her eyes leaving no doubt as to exactly what she meant. A tingle ran right up Dorsey's arm at her touch.

"Yeah, me too," she finally managed to say, finding herself momentarily tongue-tied in the face of Sarah's double entendre and Maggie's cheerful round visage innocently beaming at them both. They waved as they went out the front door.

Oh, no, Dorsey thought as they left. This was not good. For one thing, she was a terrible liar, so she always told the truth. The truth was just so much easier to keep track of. On the other hand, it had gotten her into a lot of trouble over the years. People are much more comfortable with their facts liberally sugar-coated, she'd found. She'd decided at an early age that she'd rather speak the truth or be silent. Which didn't leave her with much to say in Romeo Falls. But even if she did want to fib, she could never lie to Maggie—when you've sold Girl Scout cookies door-to-door together, presided over the marriage of your GI Joe and Barbie dolls countless times and mutually suffered through puberty, high school and small-town melodrama for twenty years, there's just no room for deception. And she didn't *want* to deceive Maggie. But this wasn't her secret to tell...

All of a sudden, her summer was looking a lot more complicated.

Shaw wandered in around four thirty to help her close. Dorsey set him to sweeping the floor. The old hardwood floors were pretty clean, but it gave him something to do and would make him look busy if Goodman showed up unexpectedly, which he was wont to do. Good was easily exasperated by Shaw, the youngest and dreamiest of the Larue siblings. Shaw wasn't lazy, but he had a tendency to lose focus if a task didn't engage him. Dorsey had encouraged him to go to the community college in Grover City after high school, but Shaw couldn't quite seem to settle to anything. As his big sister, Dorsey worried about him a little from time to time, but, in truth, Shaw seemed happy with his life. He had a job and a roof over his head and that was more than a lot of twenty-three year olds could say. She'd had no interest in going to college either, so she could hardly pester him about that.

She found herself worrying more and more about her older brother as well. Goodman seemed to get a little angrier, a little more stressed out with each passing year. He had inherited the hardware store when their father, Hollis, died several years back. Dorsey didn't mind about the store as it wasn't the future she wanted and she knew it was what Good wanted. She'd gotten everything she needed from her father when he was alive—not only had he given her his unconditional love, he'd also taught her everything she knew about carpentry and woodworking. The workshop Hollis had built behind their house was now her refuge. There, amongst the power tools and the smell of sawdust, she could indulge her hobby of "re-imagining" the antique (or just plain old) furniture she found at garage sales and curbside. In a perfect world, she would be making a living off her hobby. But Romeo Falls was far from a perfect world, in more ways than one.

She knew she had a job at the hardware store as long as she wanted one, since Good was fair-minded and generous to a fault. Despite the always uncertain incomes of farmers and the unpredictable economic times in general, Larue's Swingtime Hardware usually made a small profit. The three of them were scraping by, but only because the Larue family had owned both the store building and their house for three generations. But the new home center in Grover was a looming threat on the horizon, like a funnel cloud seen from afar on the prairie.

Sometimes, lying awake in the middle of the night, Dorsey thought about packing a bag, getting in her little pickup and just taking off for some place like Chicago or Denver. California even. Anywhere far from Romeo Falls. But she knew that was just a fantasy. She couldn't leave Good in the lurch like that. And everything else aside, taking off would mean leaving her woodworking workshop behind, which she could never imagine. Besides, she told herself on those sleepless nights, what would she do in such a faraway place, a big city, not knowing anyone? Seriously, who would hire some nonunion butch carpenter girl from the sticks? No one, that's who. So she was stuck. And you'd better get used to it, she told herself sternly.

But the loneliness was getting harder every year. She was stuck all right—stuck with no girlfriend, no sex life, not even any prospects. Besides herself, the lesbian population of Romeo Falls totaled (maybe) four. There was the old dyke couple in their seventies who'd been around so long people had almost forgotten they weren't respectable. And the town's wannabe wild child, the jailbait daughter of the Presbyterian minister, whom Dorsey didn't count despite the rumors of the girl kissing one of the cheerleaders from the rival high school. No, Dorsey suspected wild child Mariah was just a poser since she'd already worked her way through short attention-getting stints of cutting, bulimia, dying her hair magenta and professing to have both read and enjoyed Virginia Woolf. Finally, there was the new doctor in town, whom everyone was assuming was gay because she was unmarried, in her early thirties, with short hair, short nails and sensible shoes, and—worst of all—didn't socialize much. Plus, she was from Chicago, which was right next door to Sodom and Gomorrah in the eyes of most Romeo Falls residents. How the hell she had ended up in their small town was a mystery. It was widely assumed she must have been at the bottom of her med school class and/or killed several patients on the operating table. Dorsey didn't get any gay vibe from the doctor (who was definitely not her type anyway), but since no one had asked her opinion, she kept it to herself.

These gloomy and depressing thoughts were interrupted by the jangling of the bell. Shaw was slowly sweeping his way past the front door when a smirking young man came in.

"What's up, La Puke," he said nastily to Shaw.

"Hi, Justin," Shaw replied glumly. He and Justin Argyle had never been friends, despite the fact they'd gone from kindergarten all the way through high school together. Mostly because Justin was a jackass. He was the only child of a divorced woman who had taught history at the junior high school for several years. Dorsey, Maggie and Shaw had all suffered through her classes, as had Justin himself. Mrs. Argyle was quickly dubbed "Mrs. Gargoyle" by the kids, which meant that Justin was soon known throughout the county as Gargoyle, Jr.

Mrs. Gargoyle had surprised everyone by quitting her teaching position about five years back and applying for the police officer job which opened up when Luke Bergstrom—Maggie's one-time brother-in-law—was promoted to chief on the occasion of the old chief's retirement. Even more surprising was the fact that she got the job. A tall, raw-boned and ill-tempered woman, she was even more imposing in her uniform and gun belt. Not a single one of her former students had given her any lip since she got the gun. But they still called her Mrs. Gargoyle behind her back. Her son, Justin, who had been in and out of trouble since he was thirteen, still lived with his mother.

Now, as he headed down one of the aisles, Dorsey and Shaw exchanged a look. Justin was about as trustworthy as a snake, so Shaw moved over to sweep the floor at the head of that aisle, keeping his distance but vigilant for any attempt at shoplifting. Justin was back out again in a minute, though, and headed toward Dorsey at the cash register.

"How's it going, Justin?" she said evenly.

He shot her a look in which dislike was ill-concealed and said nothing. He slapped a single item down on the counter—a red plastic "wand" lighter of the type used for lighting grills and candles—and rummaged in the pocket of his dirty jean jacket for some money.

In another attempt at pleasant conversation, which was totally wasted on Gargoyle, Jr., Dorsey asked, "You and your mom doing a little barbecuing this summer?"

He shrugged irritably. "Whatever. How much?"

She rang up the purchase and took his crumpled bills, then gave him the change and receipt.

"Would you like a bag for that?"

He shook his head impatiently and stuffed his change and the receipt in the pocket of his grubby jacket. He grabbed the lighter and headed for the door, sneering at Shaw who was standing well out of his path with the broom clutched to his chest.

"Well, you say hi to your mother for me!" Dorsey hollered after Justin, not meaning a word of it. The door clanged shut behind him, the bell jangling one last time for the day. Dorsey's gaze met Shaw's and they both burst out laughing at the one-sided exchange.

"What a doofus," Shaw said.

"Yep," his sister agreed. It was two minutes past five on a Saturday evening. "Let's call it a day," she said. Shaw turned the cardboard sign on the door to CLOSED and locked the door.

Late that night, a solitary, dark-clad figure silently approached the highway department's big green sign just outside of town. Entering Romeo Falls, Pop. 3,557, it said in large white characters. Casting a furtive glance in all four directions, the figure dug deep into an inside jacket pocket. A shaky flashlight beam and the distinctive clanking sound of a can of spray paint being shaken disturbed the still, pitch-black night. Two long bursts, then some quick detail work. The artist paused to consider the results. Yeah. Done. The spray paint can was capped, the flashlight shut off. Then, without a backward look, the dark figure slunk off into the night, toward the lights of town.

CHAPTER THREE

The vandalism was the talk of the town on Sunday morning. Someone had crossed out the word "Falls" on the big green highway sign and spray-painted "FAILS" next to it. In red spray paint. Dorsey heard all about it when she arrived a little early at the Blue Duck Café to secure a table for herself, Maggie, Sarah and Mrs. Bigelow. The post-church brunch crowd was abuzz with speculation about the misdeed and who might have perpetrated it. The finger of suspicion seemed to point most firmly at Mariah Reinhardt, the minister's seventeen-year-old wild child, since she'd been caught red-handed the previous summer painting the F-word on the water tower. But Mrs. Reinhardt claimed her troublesome daughter had been home all night, in bed with a cold. Or so the gossips said.

Dorsey sat alone at a table for four, surrounded by the

chattering townsfolk. She felt remote from them and yet at home amongst them, the contradiction that defined her life in Romeo Falls. Whoever had defaced the sign had her sympathy. Romeo Fails, indeed.

"Coffee, Dorsey?" The waitress handed Dorsey a menu and laid three more at the empty places.

"No, thanks, Penny, the water's fine for now. The rest of them should be here any minute."

"Okay, just let me know if you need anything."

As usual, Dorsey tried to not check out Penny's impeccable ass as she headed back to the kitchen. And failed. She hoped she'd been discreet. The waitress's folks owned the restaurant. At thirty-six, Penny Bergstrom was unquestionably the most beautiful woman in the county, an opinion Dorsey shared with most of the women and all of the men in Romeo Falls. Penny had gone to school with Goodman and was married (to the chief of police, no less) with two kids. The short skirt she was wearing that day was worth the price of brunch all by itself, Dorsey thought as she perused the menu.

"Dorsey!"

A smiling Maggie was bearing down on the table, her mother and Sarah behind her. Greetings were exchanged as they sat down. The two Bigelows were decked out in their Sunday best, Maggie in a flowered dress and her mother in a pale yellow suit. Matching purses and heels went without saying for both women. Mrs. Bigelow had always somehow reminded Dorsey of Mrs. Potato Head—not that the woman looked like a spud, it was more in the fierce accessorizing which dominated her every outfit. Even working in the garden, Vivian would be sure to sport matching gloves, hat and trowel.

Sarah was elegantly low-key in a navy pinstripe pantsuit, which brought out the piercing blue of her eyes. No makeup, which was fine with Dorsey—she didn't see how any cosmetic could enhance the gorgeous cheekbones, the gracefully feathered brows, the immaculate fair skin and those amazing eyes. She definitely preferred low maintenance to high in every way. In light of Sarah's revelation about not being out to her family, Dorsey took another and more assessing look at her clothes.

Her initial reaction had simply been one of appreciation. And attraction, she admitted to herself, although she was trying hard to be cool and objective. Despite that one magical night by the lake, she hadn't sensed any interest from Sarah in rekindling anything. But back to Sarah's appearance—if it hadn't been for that night by the lake, would she have known Sarah was gay when she met her at the hardware store? She thought so, but maybe her prior knowledge and physical reaction were overriding all her other senses. Sarah was definitely more on the femme end of the scale, which no doubt made it easier for her to pass with her family. But those kinds of labels always led to confusion in Dorsey's experience. Labels could be used just as easily to reveal or conceal. Even a woman who fit the butch stereotype as well as she did had her own quirks, her own likes and dislikes. People were just people, Dorsey thought. Each one an individual who had to be figured out on his or her own terms.

Sarah sat down across from Dorsey as Maggie took the seat next to her best friend. Mrs. Bigelow faced her daughter. As Sarah took off her jacket to reveal a sleeveless, Mandarin-collared white shell and exceptionally well-toned arms, Dorsey felt a brief pang of disappointment that she wasn't sitting next to her, where her bare arm might—just by chance—brush Sarah's and no one would think anything of it. Wow, thought Dorsey, mentally making a face at herself—have I really sunk that low? Am I really that desperate?

Yes, she sighed internally. But perhaps it was better to be seated across from Sarah, she decided. That way she got to look at her, at least. And maybe gain a little insight into what was going on inside that head. Sarah looked up from studying her menu and caught Dorsey's glance. Her look was impassive, but Dorsey thought she caught a hint of warmth in the depths of those incredible blue eyes. Or did she? She was just torturing herself, she knew. And it was maddening.

"We missed you at church, Dorsey Lee," Mother Bigelow said chidingly.

And you always will, thought Dorsey, but she merely smiled neutrally at her and said nothing.

"But I guess you weren't dressed for it anyhow," Mrs.

Bigelow added, casting a disparaging eye over Dorsey's short-sleeved, brown-and-white Western-cut shirt with pearl snaps in place of buttons. Her favorite jeans and sneakers below wouldn't have garnered any praise either. The smile now rigid on her face, Dorsey gazed blindly down at her menu to avoid a response she'd only regret later. She'd learned over the years that semi-courteous silence was the most effective defense against her best friend's mother.

She felt something nudge her sneakered foot and instinctively pulled it back slightly, only to feel the nudge again. It was Sarah's foot, pressing gently against her own. She glanced at Sarah, who flicked her a look that included a small smile. She then turned her gaze back to her menu.

Dorsey felt confused. Was she flirting with her? Did she even realize their feet were touching? Was she reading something into Sarah's actions that wasn't really there? Not much liking her muddle of feelings, she sat up straight and pulled both her feet back out of range, taking a sip of her ice water in the hope it would cool her down.

The awkward moment was covered by Penny returning with the coffeepot and asking about their orders. The two Bigelow women opted for the buffet, while Sarah requested the Farmer's Combo. Dorsey went with her favorite spinach omelet. Another awkward moment soon followed, though, when Sarah asked for a mimosa. Maggie and Dorsey froze for a second, knowing Mrs. Bigelow would disapprove. The older woman was clearly gathering her forces for her usual storm of criticism, but Dorsey recovered and jumped in first.

"You know what, that sounds good," she said. "I'll have a mimosa too, please, Penny."

The quick flash of a wicked grin she got from Sarah made her heart jump in her chest. Steady, she told herself. Steady.

"Me too," piped in Maggie, surprisingly. Her mother looked like she was about to erupt, but Maggie managed to cut off the rumbling before it could begin.

"Oh, come on, Mother, it's just a little champagne—and we're celebrating Sarah being here, right?"

Vivian could hardly disagree with that, so she settled for

pushing her chair back and stalking off to the buffet line, clearly disgusted with the three of them. They waited until she was out of earshot, then dissolved into giggles like ten-year-olds. Maggie's eyes were wet behind the cloth napkin she used to dab at her eyes.

"Y'all are going to get me in trouble this summer, I can tell," she said between gasps for breath. She put the napkin down and started fanning herself with her hands instead. "Whew." Having finally collected herself, she pushed her chair back and went off to the buffet line to placate her miffed parent.

Penny was back with the three mimosas on a tray, leaning down and forward to distribute them, which was a pleasant sight in her scoop-necked T-shirt. Dorsey couldn't help but notice Sarah checking out Penny with a cool and comprehensive head-to-toe glance. She discreetly savored the rear view too as Penny departed.

"She's married," Dorsey couldn't keep herself from saying.

Sarah seemed to color slightly, but merely raised her glass to Dorsey, saying "Oh?" and meeting her level gaze with the subtlest of smiles.

"Yeah. To the chief of police."

"Oh. Well...cheers, eh?"

"Cheers," Dorsey replied.

They both took a reviving sip of mimosa. A moment of silence passed. Although they were alone at the table, Dorsey knew this was not the time for any kind of tête-à-tête as the small café was packed with her fellow townspeople. It looked like just about everybody was there that morning, from Officer Argyle in her uniform at the counter to Melba Porter, the new doctor. The physician looked uncomfortable, poor thing, as the guest of the Blankenships, he being the bank manager and she being the unofficial town welcome wagon/busybody, take your pick. The three of them were wedged in a small corner booth nearby.

Dorsey wondered when she would ever have a chance to talk with Sarah privately. Maybe it was better if she didn't, especially with the complication of Sarah not being out to Maggie. It wasn't like Sarah had made it clear she wanted to pick up where'd they'd left off that night by the lake. A couple of glances, a foot pressed against hers under the table—it was probably nothing. Probably.

"So..." Sarah said, breaking the silence. "You're the best friend I've heard about all my life."

"And you're the beloved cousin."

"I guess it's a small world," Sarah said ironically. Her gaze was more bleak than amused, though.

"Yeah, I guess."

Dorsey found herself hunting for something else to say, which was odd, considering she had about a hundred questions clamoring in her head. Like—do you ever think about that night? About me? Are you seeing anybody? In a relationship? Can we go somewhere and get naked right now?

She settled for something more appropriate to Sunday brunch.

"So...um, not to be rude, but what you are doing here exactly?" she asked.

Sarah smiled at her forthrightness. "Good question," she said. "And a long story. The short version is I'm taking some time off from work to write and I wanted to get out of the city for a while, so I decided to come visit my favorite cousin, Maggie."

That actually raised more questions than it answered, Dorsey thought.

"Taking time off to write? But don't you write for a living?" Dorsey said, a little confused. "You're some kind of reporter for a big magazine in Chicago, right?" Maggie had told her all about it, many times.

Sarah grimaced, whether at the tartness of her orange juice or at Dorsey's words, it wasn't clear.

"'Some kind of reporter'—yeah, that sounds about right," she said with a wry grin. "Or, at least it used to... I guess you could say I'm between jobs right now."

Sounds like you got fired, Dorsey thought, but was too polite to say.

"So you're spending the summer in Romeo Falls?" she ventured.

Sarah said, "Well, I don't know about the whole summer. I'm kind of playing it by ear for the moment."

"Oh." They both sipped their drinks, Dorsey wondering if Sarah was thinking about three months of Vivian Bigelow's company like she was.

"Let me ask you a question," Sarah said with a smile and neatly changing the subject, Dorsey noticed. "I've never heard of a 'swingtime' hardware store before. What's up with that?"

"Good question," Dorsey said, returning her smile and intentionally mimicking Sarah's turn of phrase. "And also a long story. I'm not sure how or why, but somewhere along the way, my father fell madly in love with swing music. You know, big band music from the forties—Benny Goodman, the Dorsey Brothers, Artie Shaw?"

"I see. And your mom let him name you after his favorite swing musicians?" Sarah's eyes lit up as she made the leap.

She was quick, this one, Dorsey thought. Smart and hot, her favorite combination.

"Yeah, you guessed it. My brothers and I all got the swing names: Goodman Armstrong, Shaw Beiderbecke and Dorsey Lee Larue."

"Lee?" Sarah queried.

"For Peggy Lee, the singer."

"Ah."

Further conversation was interrupted by the return of the Bigelow women to the table, plates laden down with buffet bounty. Mrs. Bigelow was a few steps behind her daughter, having stopped to say hello to just about everyone on the way back. Her last stop was at the Blankenship table a few feet away, where the vandalized highway sign was still the hot topic.

"So, Dorsey Lee," Mrs. Bigelow said as she sat down, having apparently decided to magnanimously forgive them all, "have the police talked to Goodman about this terrible graffiti crime?"

"To Good? I don't think so. Why would they?" Dorsey responded, surprised. No one could ever think her brother Good—salt of the earth, solid citizen, respected merchant—had anything to do with such mischief.

"Because your store is the only place in town that sells spray paint," Mrs. Bigelow replied triumphantly. Dorsey privately thought Mrs. B. had been watching too many *Murder She Wrote* reruns, but said nothing. But then Maggie jumped on the bandwagon.

"Ooh, we could be suspects, Sarah," she said with a laugh to her cousin, who was more intent on draining the last of her mimosa. "We bought some red spray paint yesterday to redo those old chairs on the porch," she told her mother, who immediately launched into a critique of Mary Margaret's crafts skills and color choices.

Sarah was looking about for their waitress, ready for another round. She located Penny behind the counter, presenting the bill to Officer Argyle. Sarah frowned as she watched that bastion of the law stand, hike up her heavy gun belt and lumber toward the cash register. Her frown was almost bordering on a glare, Dorsey observed with surprise.

"You must have met Mrs. Gargoyle," she said to Sarah. Sarah looked confused until Dorsey nodded toward the officer.

"Mrs. Garg—oh, yeah, Officer Argyle, I get it. Yeah, she welcomed me to town with a speeding ticket the other night as I drove in. I think I was doing all of thirty-seven in a thirty-five mile an hour zone. I tried to sweet talk her into just giving me a warning, but she wouldn't budge."

"She's immune to sweet talk."

"Sweet talk? Who's getting sweet talked?" Maggie chimed in with interest, picking up on Dorsey's words.

"I was just saying Mrs. Gargoyle is immune to it."

Mrs. Bigelow said with asperity, "I do wish you girls wouldn't use that horrible nickname for Gretchen. It's very rude. And un-Christian, Mary Margaret. Besides, she and Luke and the rest of them do a very good job of keeping our little town safe. Much safer than Chicago, for instance. You must be so glad to be out of that horrible city, Sarah."

"Well, I'm a big-city girl, Aunt Viv, so you know I love Chicago. Every place has its good points and bad points, I'm sure," Sarah replied diplomatically. "Although it is great to be able to take a walk after dark and feel safe here," she added.

"Oh, is that where you went last night? I heard you go out after I went to bed and was wondering," said Maggie.

"Well, I never was so glad as when Mary Margaret came home from the city after college and settled back down in Romeo Falls," Mrs. Bigelow said. "There are just so many pitfalls for a young woman alone in the city. Especially in today's world."

She shuddered, no doubt imagining all those terrible pitfalls. Her daughter's MBA was gathering dust while she taught math at the high school, but Dorsey knew this was outweighed in her mother's mind by her "escape" from the evils of big-city life. She'd heard the speech before from Mrs. Bigelow on how cities were chock-full of drug dealers, vegetarians, homosexuals, Democrats, foreigners and other persons of low repute. Dorsey ignored the diatribe and put the time to better use by catching Penny's eye, requesting another round of mimosas via hand signals. Penny soon brought the drinks along with the orders for Dorsey and Sarah.

"Whoa!" Sarah exclaimed. "This is a lot of food."

They all eyed her oversized "Farmer's Combo" platter with its generous portions of scrambled eggs, sausage, hash browns and wheat toast, plus a short stack of blueberry pancakes.

"Now you know why I'm the chubby cousin," Maggie said. "If nothing else, they feed you in this town."

"Oh, Maggie, you're fine," Sarah said. "And this is fine too. I just wasn't expecting so much. But it's all good—I like a little bit of everything."

Again there was that quick flicker of a look toward Dorsey, who couldn't help but flash back to their one night together, when Sarah had, indeed, liked a little bit of everything. *Was* she flirting? Dorsey felt her face warm and knew she was blushing, but hoped everyone else would attribute it to the mimosas or the rising temperature in the busy restaurant. She took another sip and told herself to get a grip. Just because she hadn't gotten laid since that night with Sarah almost a year ago didn't mean she had to obsess over and pick apart everything the woman said. Just because she remembers you doesn't mean she wants anything more, she told herself.

"How's your mother?" Mrs. Bigelow asked her, bringing

Dorsey back to the here and now with a jerk. "Still enjoying the Florida sunshine?"

"Yes, she's fine. She loves it down there."

Dorsey's mother had remarried a couple of years after Hollis's death, to Earl Ray the fertilizer salesman. They were down south now, in a trailer by the sea.

Mrs. Bigelow never let an opportunity pass to voice her opinion.

"What she saw in that Earl Ray I will never know. When a man spends all day with fertilizer..."

"You know he's retired now, Mother," Maggie firmly redirected the conversation. "So, Dorse, how's it going with your carpentry job? Dorsey's very skilled with her hands," she added as an aside to her cousin. Heat suffused Dorsey's face again as Sarah smiled, her blue eyes focused on applying the perfect amount of syrup to her delectable-looking pancakes.

"It's no big deal," Dorsey said, feeling embarrassed for some reason to be the center of attention. She was often more comfortable with listening than talking, especially in a group situation. "I'm just fixing up the Bartholomews' deck," she told them, naming an affluent family who farmed about ten miles west of town.

"When do they get back from their cruise?" Mrs. Bigelow wanted to know.

Between Mother Bigelow and her rival Mrs. Blankenship, they had their fingers on the pulse of just about everything going on in Romeo Falls. The Bartholomews were off on a month-long Mediterranean cruise to celebrate their twenty-fifth wedding anniversary.

"A couple more weeks," Dorsey said. "I'll be done before they get back, though. I'll be out there every night this week, probably."

"Well, maybe we'll come visit you," said Maggie, meaning herself and Sarah. "We'll bring a picnic supper and show Sarah a real live farm."

Dorsey wasn't sure how much of a treat that would be, but she knew Maggie only meant well.

"Yeah and if they have a pool, so much the better!" Sarah

said, fanning herself with the little laminated card that showcased the desserts. "I heard the weatherman say this morning that it's supposed to heat up tomorrow."

"No pool, but they do have a hot tub," Maggie told her, eyes alight with fun. Clearly, she'd already begun planning the picnic in her head.

"Now, girls," Mrs. Bigelow began in a lecturing tone. "I don't think you should be having a party at someone else's house while they're away."

"No, it's okay," Dorsey said. "Mr. Bartholomew gave me the keys and told me I could use the hot tub if I wanted. I'm watering their plants while they're gone too."

"Well, how very enterprising of you," Mrs. B. sniffed, clearly disappointed that she wouldn't get to finish her sermon on Thou Shalt Not Par-tay.

They got through the rest of brunch, despite Mrs. Bigelow's propensity to dominate the conversation with her views on her five favorite topics: (1) Why Every Young Woman Needs A Man, (2) The Economy (See Previous Topic), (3) The Liberal Media Is Brainwashing Us All Straight To H-e- *-*, (4) Kids These Days! and (5) Mary Margaret's Weight, Divorce, Job, etc. Dorsey tuned the old harpy out as best she could and divided her attention amongst the excellent food, replies whenever Maggie engaged her in the conversation and occasional glances at Sarah across the table. Her bare arms, pale, slender fingers and soft black hair were all entrancing. She had to be careful not to get lost in contemplation of the erstwhile Goddess, however—she didn't want to cause problems for Sarah, herself or anyone else. A couple of times, she found Sarah's eyes composedly regarding her from across the table. Dorsey wondered what she saw.

Mrs. Bigelow insisted on picking up the check, for which Dorsey was grateful. She hung back, though, as the rest of them headed toward the exit and covertly slipped a few extra bills onto the table. Mrs. B. was a notoriously bad tipper. While Mrs. Bigelow paid the bill, the three younger women walked outside to the parking lot for a breath of fresh air. It was a beautiful spring day with the temperature in the high sixties and a light breeze. A perfect cornflower blue sky stretched above them, with not a cloud in sight, although thunderstorms were a possibility for later in the day.

"You walking, Dorse?" Maggie asked, scanning the parking lot for her friend's little pickup truck.

"Yeah, I'm due at the hardware store in a bit. And then I might put in a few hours on the Bartholomews' deck this evening if the weather holds up. What are y'all up to today?"

"Errands, mostly," said Maggie. "And we're going to the movies in Grover City this afternoon."

"That reminds me," said Sarah. "I phoned in a prescription yesterday and I need to pick it up at the drugstore. Can we swing by there first?"

Maggie and Dorsey exchanged looks of mild dismay. Sarah appeared taken aback by their reaction.

"What?" she said.

"You phoned in a prescription? Where was I?" said Maggie.

"I don't know, in the shower, I guess," Sarah replied. "What's wrong?"

"Honey, this is a small town. And in a small town, everybody knows your business. We should have taken you over to GC to drop that off."

"But isn't the pharmacist bound by some kind of confidentiality oath?" Sarah asked.

Dorsey snorted, then mumbled "Sorry" as Sarah looked at her. Maggie continued to explain.

"The pharmacist is, yes, but his wife isn't and neither is anyone else who works in the drugstore. And somehow, sooner or later, things have a way of always getting out in this town."

"Well, I don't care," said Sarah, a little defiantly. "It's too late now anyhow and it's not like it's anything I'm ashamed of." Although she did, in fact, look a little unsettled. Maggie gazed at her with concern.

Sarah said, "I mean, hell, half the women I know in Chicago are on Prozac and proud of it. Not that I am," she added hastily, seeing the alarm on her cousin's face. "My prescription is just, uh...well, to help me sleep, mostly. It's okay, Maggie, really, it's no big thing."

"Okay," Maggie said, sounding not entirely convinced. "I

just don't want people to get the wrong idea about you. Dorse, you remember what happened with Velma Ray?"

Dorsey laughed, but said, "Look, I've got to go to work, but I'm sure you'll tell Sarah all about it. And I like your idea of a picnic—how about Wednesday?"

The three of them agreed on Wednesday night at seven for their picnic at the Bartholomew farm. Dorsey took her leave of them and headed the few blocks downtown to the hardware store. She had to smile as she heard Maggie start to tell Sarah the story in her usual highly animated way.

"There was quite the scandal when word got out that Velma Ray—she's the twin sister of the Earl Ray we mentioned earlier who married Dorsey's mom?—well, anyhow, word got out somehow that Velma Ray was on steroids. Which was ridiculous, because she's just a tiny little wisp of a thing. So, turned out it wasn't steroids, it was actually just thyroid medication and whoever started the rumor just got the 'roid' part mixed up, but even so..." Her voice faded in the distance.

By closing time, the day had turned dark and the front window of the hardware store was streaked with rivulets of rain. Thunder rumbled off in the plains as the storm moved eastward. Ira, the smaller of the two store cats, sat twitchy-tailed and wide-eyed on the counter, flinching a bit with each flash of lightning outside. George, the big surly gray, was asleep in the back on a pile of plumbing supply catalogs.

It had been a slow afternoon, thanks to the rain. Two customers and only one of them had bought something. Dorsey ran a hand through her hair impatiently, feeling a bit frustrated and antsy. The storm had ruined her plan to put in a few hours on the Bartholomew deck project, so it looked like the highlight of her evening was going to be laundry. Whoopee.

She stood at the front window of the store, watching the rain. It was dark enough outside that her reflection stared back at her in the window. Her reflection looked irritated too. She pushed an errant strand of her hair out of her green eyes for the hundredth time that day. Not a conventional beauty by Romeo Falls standards, she nonetheless had her mother's regular features and fair skin. Her height and lithe build she got from the old man, as did Shaw. Goodman, the eldest at thirty-six, was a throwback to some distant Larue—a big bear of a man with an unruly thatch of reddish brown curls and a beard to match.

Good had been in the office all afternoon, struggling with the books as the end of the month neared. Knowing how grouchy that usually made him, Dorsey had given him a wide berth for most of her shift. At one minute past five, she locked the front door and fed the cats their dinner. She finished all the other closing-up-shop tasks, then spent an hour or so restocking some shelves she hadn't got to earlier. On her way out the back, she stopped by the office to let her brother know she was leaving.

"Good?" She knocked tentatively on the frame of the office door to get his attention. "I'm taking off now, okay?"

It didn't look like he had made much headway with the books. Invoices and other paperwork littered the desk. A calculator and an adding machine held down stacks of more papers. Good had his head in his hands and was chewing on a pencil. He sat up, glancing at his watch, then leaned back and stretched.

"Yeah," he agreed, sounding tired and frustrated. "I'm getting nowhere with these books anyhow."

"You need an accountant," Dorsey said, knowing what his answer would be.

"Can't afford it," Good promptly replied. Dorsey mouthed the words along with him. He shook his head at her, then laughed out loud. He stood and started clearing up the books and papers on his desk.

"Look, you want to go get a beer at The Hamlet?" he said. "My brain is fried. I'll even buy the first round. I think I can still afford that, as long as you get something domestic."

"Well, yeah," she said, both surprised and gladdened by his suggestion. He had been so grumpy lately she couldn't remember the last time she'd shared a beverage or a meal with her oldest brother. He was always too busy with the store.

As they walked the two blocks over to the sole bar within

Romeo Falls' city limits, the rain had dissipated to just a few random drops. Blue sky was reappearing through some gaps in the cloud cover. The air felt clear and fresh. Main Street was deserted as they crossed it, dodging puddles, to make their way toward the cheerfully blinking neon lights of The Hamlet. Mrs. Gargoyle rolled slowly by in her police cruiser, then stopped as she came abreast. She lowered her window.

"Goodman. Dorsey Lee." She blew a small bubblegum bubble, then popped it loudly. Everyone knew Luke wouldn't let her smoke in the patrol car.

"Evening, Officer," Goodman amiably hailed her. "Looks like the rain's clearing up for us."

"Too bad—I wish it would keep raining," she retorted combatively. "Keeps the troublemakers off the streets, if you know what I mean, especially with school out. Can you believe when I got home last night, some little hoodlum had chopped the heads off every single one of my carnations? You know, the pink-and-white ones that line my front walk? Damn kids," she added, under her breath. "I swear, sometimes it seems like switching from the junior high school to this job was no change whatsoever."

Goodman and Dorsey expressed their condolences for the carnations.

"Well, I guess it could have been worse," said Mrs. Gargoyle philosophically. "At least the little bast—I mean, uh, rascal took the flower heads with him or her, so I didn't have to clean up anything. Damn kids," she said again, shaking her head. "They'll be sorry when I catch them, that's for damn sure."

"Any clues?" Good asked.

"No, but I've got my suspicions," she said darkly.

"How about that other thing?" Dorsey said. "The vandalized sign out on the highway?"

"The chief's working that one himself at the mayor's request," Gargoyle said, rather pompously, Dorsey thought. "It's a misdemeanor to deface government property. Plus, it makes the town look bad. What if tourists saw our sign looking like that? They'd probably keep right on going to Grover."

What tourists? Dorsey thought.

Mrs. Gargoyle continued, "I'd love to see somebody go to

jail for that, I surely would." She chomped on her gum with extra vigor to emphasize her deep feelings on the matter.

"So who did it?" asked Good.

"Luke'll find out," Gargoyle said with confidence as she raised her window and slowly cruised off.

"The Crime of the Century," Goodman said sardonically to his sister as they entered the bar.

"Which one?" Dorsey replied with a laugh. "Her flowers or the highway sign?"

"Take your pick."

The Hamlet was uncharacteristically busy for a Sunday evening, especially a rainy one. Maybe the rain had canceled other people's plans like it had hers, Dorsey thought. As Good headed to the bar to get them a couple of draft beers, she grabbed the only open table, a booth right by the front door. There were only two other booths. The one next to her was occupied by four women with whom she'd gone to school, although they'd been a few years ahead of her: Courtney Flugelmeyer, Tanya Hartwell and two of the Lucchese sisters. All had been mainstays of the 4-H club in their day. They were smoking and laughing loudly. They looked more than a little drunk. Pitchers of beer—one full, one at half-mast and one empty—crowded their table, along with the remains of a pizza, which was the new house specialty. The owner had installed a pizza oven around the first of the year and so far, it was a big hit—the next closest pizza parlor was in Grover City. Dorsey sat down in her booth on the side farthest from them, her back to the front door, hoping they were too tipsy to notice her. The third booth was taken by two local farmers and their wives, having a night on the town by the looks of things. The air was warm with the smell of booze, pizza, cigarettes and damp flannel.

Police Chief Luke Bergstrom, in jeans and a T-shirt, was playing pool with some guys from the grain elevator. The pool table took up most of the floor space in the small tavern. Besides the booths lining the front windows and the pool table in the middle, a bar ran the length of the room in the back, paralleling the booths. Seated at one end of the bar was Justin Argyle in his dirty jean jacket, morosely nursing a bottle of Coors. An empty seat separated him from some college boys, home for the summer. Country music was playing on the jukebox, but the sounds of many different conversations and the crack of the cue ball relegated it to the background.

Good set down two tall chilled glasses of beer on the table, then slid into the other side of the booth.

"Thanks, Good."

"Cheers," he said. They both took a long and fortifying swig.

"You know, Maggie could help you with those books," Dorsey said, knowing how much he hated to ask for help.

Good shook his head, frowning. "I'm sure she has a lot better things to do with her time than that. No, I'll figure it out on my own. I always do, sooner or later."

A cool gust of air blew down the back of Dorsey's neck as someone came in the bar.

"Speaking of Maggie," Good said, "isn't that her cousin?"

Dorsey half-turned in her seat. Sure enough, Sarah stood there in the entryway, a few raindrops glistening on her leather jacket and the lenses of her glasses. Her nose was wrinkled as she surveyed the dim room, although it was unclear whether that was due to the cigarette smoke, the people, the music or The Hamlet itself.

"Sarah!" Dorsey raised her voice to be heard over the noise of the bar.

Sarah turned in surprise at hearing her name. Her face lighted as she saw Dorsey sitting there. She crossed the few steps to their booth.

"Hey, Dorsey," she said. "I didn't expect to see you here."

"Sarah, this is my brother Goodman. Good, meet Sarah."

Good stood up to shake her hand. "Nice to meet you, Sarah. Welcome to Romeo Falls. I think I saw you at the market with the Bigelows earlier."

An attractive young woman in town was bound to garner attention. The grapevine must be quivering with the news, thought Dorsey. And if Good knew who she was, then everyone must know.

"Nice to meet you, Goodman."

"Would you like to join us?" he said, gesturing at Dorsey's side of the booth. At six foot three and two hundred and fifty pounds, clearly no one else would fit on his side.

"Oh, I don't want to intrude..." Sarah began, casting an uncertain glance at Dorsey.

"No, please join us," said Dorsey with a smile, scooting back to make room. "Oh... unless you're meeting someone else?"

"No," Sarah said with a laugh and to Dorsey's great relief. She slid into the booth next to her, slipping out of her leather jacket to reveal the same sleeveless blouse she'd been wearing at brunch. It looked good with her jeans, Dorsey thought. Goodman was still on his feet, being a gentleman, although he looked more like a lumberjack in his beard and his bulk and his denim shirt.

"Can I get you a beer?" he asked politely.

Sarah smiled sweetly at him and said, "How about a glass of white wine instead?"

Good hustled off to get it, apparently not impervious to the newcomer's charms. Dorsey didn't like that thought much.

"Your brother seems nice," Sarah said to Dorsey, who merely nodded while taking a sip of her beer.

"And kind of cute too, if you go for the Mountain Man look," Sarah added with a grin.

"Do you?" Dorsey asked her, suddenly wondering if Sarah was bisexual or bi-curious or whatever people were calling it these days.

"Me? No. Definitely no," Sarah said firmly. She leaned in for a moment to speak directly into Dorsey's ear. Her breath was warm on her neck, her arm pressing lightly against Dorsey's breast. "I like girls, Dorsey. Just like you." She leaned back, a smile playing about her lips, her blue eyes sparkling.

Again with the possible double meaning, Dorsey thought with more than a hint of frustration. 'Just like you' meaning 'I like girls just like you do'? Or 'I like girls who are just like you'? Why couldn't she just be clear... Or maybe she was clear and Dorsey couldn't read the signals. Frankly, she often found other lesbians completely incomprehensible. Not that she knew many. She just wished she could figure out the secret handshake, or the magic password or whatever it was that allowed other gay women to communicate with ease, instead of always being the one left wondering... All she could do was go with her usual direct and honest approach, not that it had worked particularly well in the past. She took another sip of her beer to cover her confusion, then flicked a sidelong glance at Sarah, who was examining her surroundings with interest.

Good returned with her glass of wine and eased himself back into the booth.

"So where's Maggie?" he asked Sarah, looking around to see if Maggie had come in while he'd been at the bar.

"She and Aunt Viv have some kind of meeting tonight. Quilt circle or barn raising or something," she said jokingly, rolling her eyes a little bit.

"Quilt circle sounds more plausible," Good said dryly.

"Yeah, I guess so. They invited me to go, but honestly, I needed some alone time. Don't get me wrong, I love Mags and Aunt Viv to death, but I'm used to spending a lot of time by myself. Of course, then I remembered there's not a drop of booze to be found in Aunt Viv's house. So when it stopped raining, I thought I'd take a walk and see if I could find a place to have a glass of wine somewhere."

"Well, you found it," Dorsey said. "The only bar in Romeo Falls."

"The Hamlet," Sarah said. "So is this town full of Shakespeare references? I haven't noticed any others."

"Nope, this is the only one. And I don't think the owners meant it as such when they named it The Hamlet. It just turned out that way."

Good intoned, "Two beers or not two beers..."

Dorsey joined him on the punch line. "That is the question." They clinked their glasses together. Sarah laughed, more at their interaction than the lame joke. She took a small sip of her wine, then wrinkled her nose again as smoke from the 4-Hers' booth eddied over their table.

"Sorry about that," said Good, waving a big hand in the air as if that would chase away the smoke. "You're from Chicago, right? I hear you can't smoke in the bars up there anymore, is that right?"

"That's true. That's one thing I hate about small towns. Oh, sorry!" Sarah caught herself with a rueful grin. "That came out kind of rude. I'm sorry—Romeo Falls is lovely, really. I've always wanted to come here. I heard so much about it when I was a kid from Maggie that I kind of pictured it like...like...I don't know, like a perfect little slice of heaven, I guess." She laughed, as if at herself and her childhood vision of a midwestern paradise.

"Well, I was hoping there wouldn't be feedlots in heaven," Good chuckled. "But I guess it is pretty nice. I like it, anyhow."

"What about you?" Sarah asked Dorsey, who'd gone quiet in her corner while the two of them talked. She was enjoying the chance to observe Sarah while she spoke with Good. Her slender wrists. The hint of triceps tone in her upper arm when she raised her wineglass. The way she gracefully gestured with her hands sometimes when she talked. The way the subdued lighting in the bar made subtle highlights in her soft, straight, coal-black hair. Hair she wanted to run her hands through, right there, right then...

"Dorsey?"

Dorsey realized both Sarah and Good were looking right at her, apparently expecting a reply to some question she'd missed. Before she could respond, Luke Bergstrom called out to Good to come play pool. Good gulped down the rest of his beer, made his excuses to Sarah and Dorsey, then joined Luke at the pool table.

"Who's his buddy? The big good-looking guy?" Sarah wanted to know.

"That's Luke Bergstrom, our chief of police. Husband of our waitress from brunch this morning, if you recall."

If you dug deep enough, practically everybody in Romeo Falls was somehow related to everybody else, by marriage if not by blood.

"Wait—Bergstrom? As in Maggie's ex-husband Bergstrom?"

"Right. She's divorced from Dwayne—thank God—and that's his older brother Luke, who is nothing like Dwayne, by the way. Luke and Good played football together in high school. Luke was the nose tackle and Good was the center. But I don't know if you follow football..." Dorsey trailed off.

"Are you kidding me? Da Bearz!" Sarah said with a grin, making her allegiance plain.

Courtney Flugelmeyer had noticed the two of them sitting next to each other and was staring at them with narrowed eyes. Dorsey saw Courtney elbow Tanya. Tanya looked over at Dorsey and Sarah and then said something to Courtney that made them both laugh and go back to drinking. They were doing a round of shots now and getting louder by the minute.

"So Luke and Good played football together..." Sarah prompted her, unaware of the scrutiny from one table over. She inched a little closer to hear Dorsey's reply over the barroom noise.

"Right. And hunted and fished together. Luke used to be over at our house all the time when we were kids and even when he was first on the force, but he's cut back on socializing a lot since he became chief. It must be hard for him," she mused.

"And how about your socializing?" Sarah asked. "Is that hard for you?" Her knee brushed Dorsey's under the table.

"What do you mean?" Dorsey said, a little wary of this personal turn to the conversation.

"Well, you know, small town... not a lot of fish in the pond..."

Dorsey silently eyed her over the rim of her beer glass as she drained it. Sarah looked steadily back at her for a moment, then broke the eye contact to look away.

"Oh, hell," Sarah said. "I so suck at this."

She looked back at Dorsey and said, "I guess I'm just wondering if you're seeing anyone right now."

"No, I'm not," said Dorsey. "Are you?"

"No," said Sarah. She smiled as a reciprocal slow grin appeared on Dorsey's face. There was a brief pause.

Then Dorsey said, "So now what?"

Sarah laughed. "Oh, crap," she said. "I was hoping you'd know."

"Well, are you hungry?" Dorsey tried. "'Cause I'm starving. I haven't had anything to eat since brunch."

They decided to order a pizza.

"You're not a vegetarian, are you?" Dorsey asked Sarah. Not

that she disapproved of such a healthy habit—she just wanted to make sure she didn't order something that Sarah wouldn't like.

"No," Sarah told her. "And I don't require anything fancy, either. A medium supreme will be just fine. I like a little of everything, remember? And I'll get us some more drinks while you order the pizza, all right?"

"Deal."

Dorsey went to the end of the bar where the cook waited to take her order, while Sarah spoke with the bartender. She looked awfully good in those jeans, Dorsey thought. She watched her walk back to their booth with the drinks. Luke was watching her as well. He and Good had apparently finished their game. Her brother caught her eye and came over to her.

"I'm taking off," he said. "Do you need a ride?"

"No, I'll walk. Thanks again for the beer, Good."

"Yeah, we should do that more often." He smiled and headed out the door. She turned to go back to the booth, but was forestalled by the college boys moving past her, with Justin Argyle in their midst. One of the guys was teasing him. They'd all gone to school together.

"Does your mama know you're out past your bedtime, Justin?"

"Fuck off," Justin told him. He looked like he'd had one too many.

Dorsey let them pass, then followed in their wake as they walked toward the exit. Luke was standing by the booth now, talking to Sarah. Justin bumped into him as he passed. Luke put out a stabilizing hand.

"Whoa, careful there!" he said to Justin, who shook him off impatiently.

"Lemme go," he muttered irritably, then stumbled on out the door. Luke watched him go with a frown. The last of the college boys assured Luke that they would see Justin home safely. Luke told him to drive safely, then turned back to his conversation with Sarah, who was looking a little irritated herself.

"Hi, Luke," Dorsey said. "Are you joining us?" She hoped the answer was no, but didn't want to be rude.

"Hey there, Dorsey. Don't mind if I do, for a minute."

He slid into the side of the booth across from Sarah, setting his red plastic cup of soda down on the table. Dorsey sat down next to her.

"I guess you two have met," she said to Sarah.

Sarah nodded, although not with great enthusiasm, Dorsey noticed.

"Pizza will be here shortly," Dorsey told her. Sarah nodded again.

"Ah, yes, the famous cousin from the big city who wasn't at the wedding," Luke said with a grin. "I was the best man," he told Sarah. "It about broke Maggie's heart that you couldn't make it."

Sarah grimaced with regret. "I know, I felt awful about that, but my editor had me on assignment in London and I couldn't get back for the ceremony. I still feel terrible about that. Maggie had even asked me to be one of her bridesmaids."

"Yeah, you missed out on some kick-ass peach chiffon dresses," Dorsey kidded her.

"Oh, really? You must've been the maid of honor, right?"

"Yep. But no dress for me. Maggie and I compromised on an equally horrifying peach pantsuit."

"Sounds sexy," Sarah said, flicking Dorsey a grin. "Now I'm doubly sorry I missed the wedding."

Dorsey grinned back at her, then shot a look over at Luke, who was unconcernedly drinking his soda and watching the two of them. She didn't think they'd gone too far (although more than far enough, probably), but Luke was no dummy. He merely gazed back at her in a friendly fashion, however.

"So, what do you think of Romeo Falls?" Luke asked Sarah, turning his attention back to her. "How does it compare with Chicago?"

"It's awesome," Sarah said shortly.

Dorsey caught no hint of sarcasm in her tone, but her cursory reply seemed intended to cut Luke short. Dorsey's leg brushed against Sarah's under the table—she could feel the tension in Sarah, but wasn't sure of the reason for it. Luke, however, seemed undeterred by her terse response.

"And what brings you to town?" he asked.

"Oh, I had some time on my hands and wanted to visit Maggie."

"How long are you staying?"

Sarah cocked her head to one side and considered him for a moment. "You ask a lot of questions, Luke."

"Sorry," he said, holding up his hands placatingly "Occupational hazard. And I'm afraid I have one more question, but this one's for Dorsey."

"What is it?" Dorsey said.

"Have you sold red spray paint to anyone lately?"

Sarah froze in the middle of lifting her wineglass to her lips, but then recovered so that the motion almost looked uninterrupted. Almost.

There was a split second when Dorsey thought about not telling Luke about Maggie and Sarah buying the red paint the day before. But that was crazy. What was she thinking? Why would she lie to Luke for no reason whatsoever? It wasn't like buying the paint implicated either of them. That was just silly.

"Well, actually, Maggie and Sarah bought some yesterday. Maggie said she wanted to redo her porch chairs."

Dorsey looked to Sarah for corroboration. Sarah merely nodded while taking another sip of wine.

"Oh and I remember Dr. Melba bought some spray paint a while back. Couple of months ago, maybe. But I'm not sure if it was red," Dorsey said. "Goodman rang up the purchase if I recall correctly. I suppose you're asking Good and Shaw this same question?"

Luke nodded. Having pointed a finger at Sarah—sort of— Dorsey now felt obliged to stand up for her.

"But Luke, anyone could have a can of red spray paint. They could have bought it six months or a year ago, or in Grover. Or Timbuktu, for that matter!"

"I know," he said. "But just because a question's obvious doesn't mean you shouldn't ask it."

While the two women considered that in silence, the bartender arrived with their pizza and a couple of plates.

"Thanks, Kenny," Dorsey said. "Can we get another round when you have a moment?"

"Sure thing, Dorsey."

Luke stood up and said, "Well, I'll leave you ladies to your pizza. I've got some more pool to play. Sarah, it was nice to meet you."

Sarah nodded and smiled at him, but Dorsey thought her smile looked a little forced. Sarah's eyes were pinned on Luke's broad back as he returned to the pool table, where the Lucchese sisters were currently trying to play, hampered by blood alcohol levels probably well over the legal limit.

"You okay?" she said to Sarah.

Sarah gave herself a little shake as if to release tension, then smiled brightly back at Dorsey.

"Sorry," she said. "I'm not a big fan of cops."

Dorsey noticed that Courtney and Tanya, who were still seated in their booth, were now muttering to each other, while giving her and Sarah some hard looks. With a sigh, Dorsey got up and moved to the other side of the table.

"Seriously?" Sarah said to her. She seemed disappointed that Dorsey had opted to sit elsewhere. She didn't appear to have picked up on the vibe from the next booth.

"The natives are restless," Dorsey replied in a quiet voice that she hoped Sarah would hear, but the next booth would not. Sarah arched an eyebrow and looked around the room, then shrugged. Maybe she was used to it, Dorsey thought. Or maybe it was easier to take coming from strangers instead of people you'd known your whole life.

Kenny the bartender brought another beer and a glass of wine as they enjoyed the pizza, which was deliciously hot and loaded with toppings.

"Oh my God, this is so good, but I'm full," bemoaned Sarah, three slices later.

Dorsey smiled at her obvious despair that she couldn't stuff a fourth slice down her throat. At least she wasn't one of those girls who ate like a bird, complaining all the while about calories and carbohydrates. It dawned on her that she was having a really good time. That was such an unusual sensation, she wasn't used to it. She was feeling a little nervous, though, for at least two reasons. Where was this going, exactly? Anywhere? She tried to tell herself to just relax and enjoy the moment. But reason number two was hampering her efforts in that area—the mutters from the booth behind her had gotten louder as the evening progressed. She'd already heard one full-volume "fuckin' dykes" from Courtney. She knew they should probably leave before things got ugly, but she hated letting them chase her out. And, from a practical standpoint, they were probably safer inside the bar with the chief of police ten feet away than they would be outside in the parking lot. Tanya, especially, was known in high school to be both a biter and a spitter. Based on long experience, Dorsey found both her and Courtney to be despicable, ignorant, fearful women. One was vice president of the PTA. The other taught Sunday school at the Presbyterian church. Pillars of the community.

Sarah pushed the decimated pizza platter aside and reached for Dorsey's hand, taking her by surprise. She didn't pull away, although she knew she should in that public place. Maybe, at twenty-six, she was finally reaching that "they can all go to hell" stage, she thought. Or maybe it was because it was Sarah, whose hand was warm on hers.

"So..." said Sarah, giving her a searching look and the full effect of those amazing blue eyes.

"So..." said Dorsey, feeling a little light-headed from the beer and the contact. Not necessarily in that order.

There was a commotion behind her. Dorsey heard more than saw glasses being knocked over, cursing and a not-so-muffled shout that sounded something like, "Goddamn homos trying to take over our town..."

Pulling her hand out of Sarah's, Dorsey whipped around in the booth in time to see Luke stroll up to the women next door and say, "Evening, ladies. Everything okay here?"

Courtney was on her feet, as were the Luccheses, who had rushed over to restrain her. Tanya was sprawled sideways in the booth trying to staunch the flow of beer from an overturned pitcher and various glasses. Dorsey couldn't make out their mumbled replies to Luke, but, after a moment, all four of them headed off to the restroom. Courtney was still squawking, but the Lucchese sisters had her in a firm grip. She shot Dorsey an evil look over her shoulder as they disappeared down the hallway.

Dorsey turned around to see how Sarah was reacting to all this. The smile on her lips and the slant of her eyebrows looked more amused than alarmed.

Luke slid into the booth next to Dorsey and said, "Maybe you should give it a rest, Dorsey."

"*I* should give it a rest?" she responded, outraged. "What the hell did I do?"

"Come on," he said. "I'm just trying to keep the peace here. You know they're not ready."

Dorsey said bitterly, "Well, when will they be ready, Luke? Exactly how long am I supposed to wait?"

"I don't know," he replied seriously. "But we're making progress."

She snorted derisively. "Progress."

"Open your eyes, Dorsey, and think about it," he admonished her. "It's slow, I know, but it's there. When your grandfather opened the hardware store, this town never thought we'd see an African American teacher and now there's Rick."

Rick Caldwell was the assistant principal at the high school.

Luke went on. "And when my dad got home from Vietnam, he sure never thought there'd ever be a female police officer in Romeo Falls."

He and Dorsey exchanged wan smiles as they imagined what his father, a hell-raising marine of the old school, would have made of Mrs. Gargoyle.

"So I don't know when they're going to be ready, Dorse. But I believe it will be in our lifetime. Even here, in this slowpoke little town that sometimes forgets you're one of us. But for tonight..."

His voice trailed off and he glanced over at the booth vacated by the drunken 4-Hers, then looked back at Dorsey and Sarah with a grin. "For tonight, you're about to get your asses kicked in the parking lot of The Hamlet. So, will you please let me drive you home and we can all have a peaceful Sunday night? Please?"

Dorsey, still feeling a little belligerent, mostly thanks to the three beers she'd had, said, "If you think we're going to ride in the back of your squad car like criminals, Luke Bergstrom, you must be out of your damn mind!"

"I'm off-duty, genius," he said, looking at her with exasperation tinged with fondness, "in case you hadn't noticed the plain clothes. I've got the minivan tonight. And I have to go pick up Penny and the kids at her mom's in about fifteen minutes, so that's just enough time for me to run you and Sarah home."

Dorsey hated the idea of retreating from the battlefield, so to speak, but Sarah chimed in for the first time since Luke had rejoined them.

"Thanks, Luke," she said smoothly. "We'd love a ride."

The three of them had been silent during the short ride from The Hamlet to the Bigelow house. What was there to say anyhow, Dorsey thought. Alone in the dark backseat of the minivan—littered with toys, a child seat, dog hair and random Cheerios—she felt like she'd been wrenched from a really good dream back into her dreary reality. Sheet lightning flickered off in the distance, briefly illuminating the now black night sky. The thunder that followed was so long in coming, the two events seemed unconnected.

Luke stopped and Sarah got out, then leaned back in the open passenger door to say goodnight to him. She glanced in the back, raking Dorsey with her gaze. Her eyes gleamed in the darkness. No word passed between them, but Dorsey felt a shock at the impact of that gaze. She suddenly felt like she couldn't breathe in the car. She scrambled out the side door, calling a thanks over her shoulder to Luke, saying she'd walk home from there. He drove off, his taillights winking at the corner as he turned and then pulled out of sight.

She and Sarah stood alone on the sidewalk. A street lamp at the corner cast a modest glow. No one else was around, though lights in the neighborhood houses reminded them they were not the only ones there. Sarah's Bug was parked at the curb. Both Maggie's car and her mother's were parked in the driveway, indicating they were both home from quilting. Lights were on, both upstairs and down.

"I guess we could go in," said Sarah. She sounded reluctant.

Dorsey knew how that would go. The bright lights, the small talk, the cooking smells, Mrs. Bigelow's stupid dog yapping nonstop... She didn't want her night with Sarah to end that way. As if they were just acquaintances. As if this feeling of electricity didn't tingle between them.

"No," she said solemnly, shaking her head.

Sarah seemed glad to have a reason not to go in just yet. She grabbed Dorsey's arm and said, "Come on—I'll walk you to the corner."

They strolled arm in arm down the block, scudding clouds alternately revealing and obscuring the quarter moon above. The wind gently ruffled the green leaves of the trees, sprinkling them with a few fat raindrops. They stopped at the corner, out of sight of Maggie's house. Dorsey slowly disengaged her arm, her fingertips lingering on Sarah's for a moment.

"This is me," she said, pointing east down the cross street, in the direction of her house.

Sarah gave her another one of those searching glances, her lips parted ever so slightly as she gazed upward at her.

"Good night, Dorsey," she said. She reached up and gave her a swift hug, which ended with an equally swift light kiss on the cheek. With Sarah's arms still around her neck and the feel of her soft lips still on her cheek, Dorsey looked into her eyes for a long moment. This is my best friend's cousin, she thought with some confusion. But this is my Silver Lake Goddess. No, this is someone I don't really know at all...

A car door slammed up the street, making her involuntarily flinch. She took two quick steps back from Sarah as she heard the engine start. Headlights flared, catching them in their beam. A pickup came slowly down the street behind them, paused at the intersection and then moved on.

Sarah looked at her with some confusion of her own, mixed with reproach, Dorsey thought.

"I—" she started.

"No, it's fine," Sarah said shortly, taking a step backward of her own. "I shouldn't have done that. Sorry."

"No, wait—" Dorsey tried again.

But Sarah was already hurrying back up the street toward

the Bigelow house. She saw Sarah go up the walk, heard the front door open and close in the clear night air. She stood there alone for a few minutes in the darkness, cursing herself, cursing Romeo Falls, wishing her life were anything but what it was.

"Good night, Sarah," she finally said out loud to nothing and nobody, feeling as if a hand were cruelly squeezing her heart. Wanting nothing more than to go grab Sarah and hold her tight, to feel her body against hers one more time. As she turned and slowly headed for home, a fine, mist-like drizzle came down, beading her head and shoulders with moisture.

CHAPTER FOUR

On Tuesday morning, Luke Bergstrom sat at his desk in the police station. Wearing latex gloves, he was examining a box wrapped in brown paper. It had been mailed to "Romeo Falls Police" in town the previous day. It wasn't heavy. Or ticking. It was about the size of a shoebox and didn't smell like anything except the paper it was wrapped in. The address label had been generated by a computer and looked completely generic. There was no return address. He hadn't fingerprinted it, but there were no identifying marks visible to the naked eye. He picked up the box and shook it gently. He could feel the contents shift inside and heard them rustle lightly. He didn't really think it was anything dangerous, but Luke was a cautious man when he had the time to be. Four years in the Marine Corps and fourteen on the force had taught him that. On the other hand, the police department did get mail and hand-delivered packages, just like everybody else. Hell, the little old ladies in this town still brought baked goods to the station for the cops. And they ate them too.

This box didn't have cookies in it, though. It didn't weigh enough for that. Luke had a funny feeling about it. He decided to take it out back to the small parking lot behind the station and open it there.

"Whatcha got there, Chief?" Officer Argyle had spotted him in the hallway with the box under his arm and was alert to the possibility of home-baked brownies in the building.

"Anonymous box someone sent us. I'm going to open it outside just in case it's something messy."

Gargoyle hitched up her belt and followed him, though she kept a safe distance as he knelt down to open it. Still wearing his gloves, he carefully removed the brown wrapping paper to reveal, as expected, a cardboard shoebox. The brand of shoes was a popular one—practically every kid in town and many of the adults were wearing that brand that year. The label identifying the size and style of the shoes had been ripped off. With his pen, Luke gently lifted the top off the box.

"What is it?" Gargoyle called.

"Come see for yourself," Luke said, picking up the box and holding it so she could view the contents. Which were a dozen carnation heads, all spray-painted black. Except for one on top, in the middle. It was painted red.

Dorsey wiped the sweat off her forehead with the sleeve of her T-shirt and decided to call it a day. The locusts were keening so loudly she could hardly hear herself think. The Bartholomews' deck was looking pretty good. A few more days and the job would be complete, in plenty of time before their scheduled return from Europe.

By the time she'd put her tools away, swept the deck and watered the plants, it was almost seven thirty. Maggie and Sarah were running late, which was odd. Maggie was the type who would always show up early so Dorsey wondered what was keeping them. She never drank on the job, but had brought a cooler with a six-pack of St. Pauli Girl beer in it for the "party." She opened one now, savoring the coolness of the green glass bottle in her hands and the cold beer on her tongue as she sat down on the steps of the deck to await the arrival of her guests.

After that debacle on Sunday night, she had wondered if the picnic plan would still be on, but Maggie had assured her on the phone that it was. She sounded the same as ever—cheerful and enthused—so apparently Sarah hadn't said anything to her. Maybe it was all for the best, Dorsey kept telling herself. Anything that involved lying to Maggie was not good. And besides—did she really think Sarah from the big city had any long-term interest in her small-town self? It was better just to view her as a new friend. A short-term friend. An acquaintance, really. Her social circle was so limited, any addition to it was to be valued.

She hadn't seen Sarah, or Maggie for that matter, since Sunday and was looking forward to seeing both of them now. Between the hardware store and the deck, she'd been busy with work. Maggie was off for the summer (one of the perks of her teaching job) and thus was free to go do whatever with Sarah. Dorsey wondered what they'd been up to. After they'd visited all the Bigelow relatives in the tri-county area, what was there to do? And where the hell were they anyhow?

She decided to change into her swimsuit in the Bartholomews' kitchen, which was just off the deck, and then fire up the hot tub. Whether Maggie and Sarah showed or not, she might as well enjoy the bubbles. Although just how enjoyable that would be all by her lonesome was debatable. And to think she'd splurged and bought a new bathing suit for this. Her old Speedo one-piece was fine for swimming laps at the community center pool, but she'd found herself wanting to look good for Sarah. What was the point of staying in shape if you couldn't show off your abs once in a while? Her daily ritual of fifty push-ups and fifty sit-ups ought to earn some reward. As she shucked off her jeans to change into her green-and-black bikini top paired with black boyshort-style bottoms, she wondered what Sarah would be wearing... Then told herself to snap out of it. This wasn't a date, she firmly told herself. Maggie was coming too. Just three friends hanging out.

She finished changing, then walked out on the deck to turn on the hot tub. She dipped a toe into the bubbles. Although the warm night air felt good on her skin, she realized she did not want to greet the other two in just her swimsuit. She pulled her jeans back on and stuck her bare feet in her unlaced work boots, in case she needed to venture out on the gravel driveway to help them unload. The sunset was spectacular off to the west, with the sun hiding behind big puffy clouds glowing pink and gold. The external lights for the house, deck and yard came on automatically as the light diminished, casting shadows amongst the large potted plants that lined the railing of the deck. The Bartholomews, who were one of the wealthier families in the area, also had a fancy automated misting system that kept the mosquitoes away. As she retrieved another "Girl Beer" (as Shaw called them) from the cooler, Dorsey heard a car pull off the highway and head up the long driveway toward the house.

"Finally!" Dorsey said out loud. It was Maggie's sensible sedan, not the cute little Bug. They pulled around to the side of the house where the large deck formed an L to the main structure. Dorsey waved to them from the top of the steps, then went down toward the car.

"Hey there, women!"

The engine was still running. The passenger door opened and Sarah got out, wearing shorts and a T-shirt. While she went to the back of the car to unload the trunk, Maggie leaned over to speak to Dorsey through the open passenger window. She looked a bit frazzled.

"Hey, Mags—what's up?"

"Oh, you are not going to believe this! Mother tripped over that stupid Carmichael just as we were getting ready to leave and hurt her ankle. It might be broken."

Carmichael was Mrs. Bigelow's elderly beagle.

"Oh, no," Dorsey said. "Is she going to be okay?"

"Well, I just left her at Dr. Melba's office, but I may have to run her over to the ER in Grover to get an x-ray. And then I had to take that damn Carmichael to the vet as well. He and Mother both went down in a heap and it looks like he may have broken his ankle too! Can you believe it?"

"Uh...do dogs even have ankles?" Dorsey wondered.

"Well, whatever the doggy equivalent of an ankle is," Maggie said shortly, uncharacteristically out of sorts. "In any event, I have to get back. But I brought Sarah and the picnic basket—there's no point in all of us having our evening ruined." She sighed, clearly unhappy with the turn of events.

Sarah had set a basket, a cooler and a beach towel down on the drive. She closed the trunk and joined Dorsey at the passenger window. As she crouched down beside her to talk to Maggie, the soft cotton of her shirt brushed Dorsey's bare side. A visceral tingle ran through Dorsey's body, releasing a shiver that was almost a shudder. She did her best to conceal her unexpected physical reaction. Be cool, she sternly told herself. But there was nothing cool about the way her body was responding to Sarah's close proximity.

"Really, Mags, maybe I should come with you," Sarah was saying. It sounded like the continuation of a prior conversation. "I can keep you company at the ER or wherever."

"Yeah, I can come too, if that will be of any help," Dorsey volunteered, although she already felt crushed with disappointment at the thought of abandoning their plans. She so rarely got to have just a fun night. Spending the evening at the Grover City emergency room—since there was no hospital in Romeo Falls—sounded utterly grim by comparison.

"No, no," Maggie said decisively. "You know how Mother gets. The more people around her, the more she'll just act up. It'll be easier, really, to deal with her by myself. Hopefully, it's just a sprain and I can just take her home when I get back to Dr. Melba's."

"What about Carmichael?" Dorsey asked, although she had zero affection for that scruffy hound. Despite the fact she'd been a regular visitor to the Bigelow house since long before Carmichael had arrived on the scene as a puppy twelve years prior, the damn dog still barked at her hysterically every time she went over. He'd also bitten Maggie twice over the years and was housebroken only when he felt like it. Lassie, he was not.

"The vet's going to keep him overnight," Maggie said. "Anyhow, I've got to run—I'll come back if I can and join you two later, so save me a beer, for heaven's sakes! I'll need one by then. But if I can't make it, Dorsey, you'll give Sarah a ride home, right?"

"Of course," Dorsey agreed.

"See you!" Maggie called as she executed a quick three-point turn and headed back into town, leaving a trail of dust behind her.

It seemed very quiet when she'd gone. Even the screeching of the locusts had died down for the moment, leaving only the chirping of crickets and the bubbling of the hot tub to fill the warm night air.

Dorsey and Sarah looked at each other.

"Wow," Dorsey said, for lack of a better word.

"Yeah, poor Mags," Sarah said, then added dutifully, "And Aunt Viv too, of course. That stupid dog... I think she was more worried about him than herself. Do you know that crazy mutt will come in my room and destroy my things if I don't put everything out of his reach? He was chewing on my hairbrush the other day. Lord only knows how he got a hold of that."

Dorsey couldn't help but smile at her. Sarah smiled back. The night seemed suddenly full of possibility.

"Look," Sarah said. "About the other night..."

"I'm sorry," Dorsey interjected, just as Sarah simultaneously said, "I'm sorry."

They both laughed then, relieved. Dorsey went on, glad to have the opportunity to share her feelings with the other girl, even if her words were tumbling over one another.

"It's just that it's a small town...and Maggie's my best friend... and with you not being out to her..."

"I know," Sarah said.

"Why aren't you out?" Dorsey heard herself blurt out involuntarily. "I'm sorry, that came out kind of rude, I guess. It's none of my business. If you don't want to talk about it, that's cool."

"No, we can talk about it," Sarah said seriously, but then grinned. "I'm pretty sure that's going to require some alcohol, though."

"Oh, of course," Dorsey said. "Where are my manners? Let's get this stuff up on the deck. And then we can talk, or I can show you around, or whatever."

"Whatever sounds good," Sarah agreed, still grinning. Between the two of them, they moved all the party supplies to the patio table at the end of the deck.

"Would you like a beer?" Dorsey asked, opening her cooler to offer her a St. Pauli Girl.

Sarah laughed and opened the cooler she had brought to reveal more St. Pauli Girl, plus a bottle of wine.

"Yeah," she said. "I'd love one of your beers."

Their fingers touched briefly as Dorsey handed her an opened bottle. It was just a little thing, the two of them bringing the same beer, but it felt like a good start to the evening.

"So—do you actually want a tour of the farm, like Maggie said?" Dorsey asked. "There's not much to see with the sun almost down, but I could show you their barn, at least. Take a picture of you sitting on the tractor that you can show all your big-city friends," she teased.

"Well, as thrilling as that sounds, after all that medical drama I'd rather just chill out in the hot tub and drink a few beers, you know what I mean?"

"Absolutely," Dorsey said. "You can change in the house, if you like."

"Oh, that's okay," Sarah said, setting her beer down and kicking off her flip-flops. "I've got my suit on underneath here."

In one swift, graceful move, she peeled off her T-shirt, leaving Dorsey breathless as she saw first the shapely curves of her stomach, then a quick glimpse of the underside of a bikini-clad breast. Dorsey's eyes followed upward from the bikini top to slender shoulders and an elegant neck.

Sarah was already taking off her shorts to reveal the bottom half of a swimsuit in radiant tones of pink, lavender and purple, much like the sunset behind her. She looked up to find Dorsey's entranced gaze locked on her. The body was everything she'd remembered from that night by the lake.

"I like your outfit too," Sarah said wryly to Dorsey, adjusting her glasses which had been knocked slightly askew by her quick change act. Her eyes slowly scanned down Dorsey's lithe frame to take in her bikini top, abs, low-slung holey blue jeans and unlaced work boots. She lazily trailed a fingertip across Dorsey's stomach as she walked past her to the hot tub. Dorsey stared after her for a second, taking in the very nice rear view, then hastily shed her boots and jeans, leaving them in a pile on the deck. Sarah was delicately dipping a toe in the water. Dorsey joined her after grabbing both their beers, the smaller of the two coolers and the bottle opener.

"How's the temperature?" Dorsey asked, handing Sarah her beer and setting the cooler and opener down at the side of the tub.

"Very nice," Sarah declared judiciously. "After you," she gestured with a graceful sweep of her arm.

Dorsey stepped in and waded to the far side. Sarah serenely sat down opposite her. To Dorsey, it felt like they were a mile apart. She tried to relax, leaning back against the side of the tub and stretching both arms out at shoulder level along the top. Now that she and Sarah were finally, totally alone, they could both speak freely. She hoped. She looked up at the first evening stars in the vast sky above them and took a big breath.

"So...you were saying?" she prompted Sarah.

"About being out?"

Dorsey nodded and took a sip of her beer.

"Aunt Viv is my mother's older sister," Sarah began slowly. "My mom moved away from Romeo Falls a long time ago, before I was born. She and Viv are not alike in a lot of ways, but my mom is very conservative. Like Viv."

There was a long pause while Sarah took a drink of her beer and seemed to be marshaling her thoughts.

"Anyhow," she continued, "let's just say it was difficult for her when I came out to my parents. My dad was pretty cool with it, once he got over the initial shock, but my mom...well, it's been a hard road for her. And me."

She looked down. Dorsey thought she looked like she might be blinking away tears. Compassion welled inside her.

Sarah shook her head as if to shake away unwelcome thoughts and went on.

"Anyway," she said, "she made me promise not to tell anyone else in the family. Not yet, at least. Not until she's ready. And I've been honoring that promise, although it's getting harder and harder." She laughed mirthlessly. "It's been five years, so far."

"Five years!" Dorsey exclaimed.

"Yeah. I told you she was having a hard time with it."

"That sucks," Dorsey said.

"Yeah, it does. Especially with Maggie. I hate having to lie to her, or hold things back from her. She probably thinks I'm here because I broke up with my boyfriend." She laughed her cheerless laugh again. "Although...I know from what Maggie's told me that she's had no problem with you being gay, but I don't know how she'll react when she eventually finds out I am. She's such a devout churchgoer, you know? Which is weird for me, because usually I can't stand religious people. They're such hypocrites. But Maggie's like a little sister to me. And when she finds out I've been keeping this from her all these years, I don't know what she'll do..."

They both contemplated this while drinking more beer. Dorsey was ready for a new one. But the cooler was on the other side, off behind Sarah's right shoulder on the deck. She cursed herself for not thinking ahead. If she stood up now, would Sarah think she was making a move on her? Should she make a move on her? Why did she always have to make things so complicated? Fuck, she thought and looked at the empty beer bottle in her hand again. She stood up abruptly, causing Sarah to look up at her questioningly.

"I, uh, need another beer," she said, simultaneously realizing that "wade" and "graceful" were two words that cannot be put together, but trying anyhow as she maneuvered across to the cooler. "How about you?"

"Thanks," Sarah murmured.

Dorsey put the two empties in the cooler, opened two new ones and passed one over to Sarah. She stood there for a moment while she tried to decide on what to say next. There was so much more Dorsey wanted to talk about with her, but she wasn't quite sure where to start. She definitely didn't want to be caught between Sarah and Maggie. That was for the two of them to work out on their own, she knew. But she didn't want to miss this opportunity to speak privately with Sarah. Who knew when they might be alone together again? Or how much time they even had that evening? Maggie might be on her way back very soon. The sky was darkening above them, with Venus and a scattering of stars now clearly visible. The moon was a bright sliver as well. She took in some air and tried to find the right words for what she wanted to say.

"We've, uh, never really talked about that night at the festival," she said, sinking down onto the seat on Sarah's side of the hot tub. Closer, but still with a good foot of space between them.

"No," Sarah agreed. There was a pause where it seemed like each was waiting for the other to speak. Sarah finally broke the silence.

"So you were working there?" she asked. That wasn't what Dorsey wanted to talk about, but maybe it was a good idea to start on safer ground.

"Yeah, I was on the crew as a carpenter, helping to set up and then break down the festival. I've done that a few times, sort of a working vacation," Dorsey said. "If you can call living in a tent in the woods for a month with a hundred lesbians a vacation. Which I do," she ended with a smile.

"Great way to meet chicks, huh?" Sarah said, her eyes twinkling.

"Not really," Dorsey replied, her smile fading. "At least, not for me. I...well, I guess I haven't had much luck in that regard, in general."

"Why not?" Sarah said. She was serious now too.

"Well, there are people who do the festival circuit all the time, you know, year in and year out. They're sort of a private club. I mean, they're friendly enough, but I always feel like kind of an outsider there. It's probably my fault...I know I'm not the most outgoing person... Anyhow, there's really no one here in town, of course. No one who's out, at least, except for the Sizzle Sisters."

"Who?"

"The Sizzle Sisters—they're not really sisters. They're these two old lesbians in their seventies who've lived together forever. I think one's a retired army nurse and the other's a retired secretary. They moved here from Grover City a long time ago. People call them the Sizzle Sisters because they've eaten dinner at the Sizzle'N'Shake every Sunday night without fail for something like the last seventeen years. You've probably seen them around town."

"Who else?" Sarah prompted.

"Nobody. Just me. There was a rumor that one of the high school girls was gay, but I'm pretty sure she started it herself, just to get attention. Oh, and some people think the new doctor is queer, but I don't get that vibe."

"Dr. Melba?" Sarah asked. "No way. Totally straight."

Dorsey felt warmed by her agreement.

"Is that it?" Sarah said.

Dorsey shrugged. "That's it. It's a small town. If there's anybody else, they're way deep in the closet."

"But...the festival..." Sarah's voice trailed off as she couldn't figure out how to end the question.

"Oh, there've been a few hook-ups along the way," Dorsey said, trying to sound casual and lighthearted. As well as not like a total loser. She really wanted Sarah to like her and she wasn't sure this cataloging of her past romantic failures was the best way to go about it. But at least they were talking. She went on.

"There was one girl I met at Festival several years ago from Albuquerque and we tried to do the long-distance thing for a while. But it didn't work out. And when I was twenty-one, there was a woman who drove a truck for one of the hardware store suppliers. Fiona... she was older...and I was young and stupid. It took me a while, but I finally figured out I was just part of her a-girl-in-every-port plan. Plus, I knew Good would be pissed if I messed up the business connection, so it was just as well that fiasco ended sooner rather than later. And then there was a highway patrol sergeant I met when she gave me a ticket a couple of years ago. But she was stationed up north in Perrinville, so that was long-distance again, plus she was way in the closet because of her job. Long story short, not meant to be."

Dorsey sighed. Her history sounded even worse out loud

than it did in her head. What a depressing and unimpressive list. What an idiot Sarah must think she was.

"Pathetic, right?" she said. She leaned back and rested her arms along the top of the tub, then took another slug of her beer.

To her surprise, Sarah slid across the space between them to sit next to her. Right next to her, in fact. Under her right arm. Their slick thighs met for a moment as Sarah reached out to briefly touch Dorsey's knee. Dorsey felt excited, yet wary—what did Sarah have in mind?

"I, uh...I haven't been totally honest with you," Sarah said quietly, looking down at the dark water bubbling beneath them. Her hands were gathered back in her lap now.

A sense of dread filled Dorsey. Instead of some mindless sex in the hot tub, or even just a pleasant conversation with another human being, clearly some kind of depressing confession would now be forthcoming. Why did these things always have to go so wrong for her, she asked herself. Why couldn't she ever find just a little piece of happiness? She felt tears pricking her eyes and angrily shook her head to clear them away.

Sarah misunderstood. "No, don't try to stop me. I need to—I want to tell you the truth."

Dorsey swallowed, her heart heavy with anxiety. Might as well get it over with, she thought.

"The truth about what, Sarah?"

"Well, I told you I'm taking some time off from work. And I am—but because I got fired."

Sarah glanced up and over at Dorsey, then back down. Dorsey could tell from her miserable gaze that this was only the beginning of the story. As fearful as she was of the ending and its implications for her, another part of her only wanted to take Sarah in her arms and tell her everything was going to be all right.

But what was everything? Clearly, more than just a lost job was going on here. Sarah was still looking down, seeming lost in reverie.

"Go on," Dorsey said to her softly, tugging gently on an upstanding spike of Sarah's coal black hair to reclaim her attention.

"There was this girl," Sarah began, sitting up a little straighter and moving closer to Dorsey in the process. Dorsey's outstretched arm hovered just over Sarah's pristine shoulders. Sarah started to speak again, then stopped, with a little laugh that was halfway to a sob. "That sounds like the first line from every piece of lesbian drama you've ever heard, right?"

"It's okay," Dorsey said calmly. "I'm listening."

"Well...her name is Ana. She was an editorial assistant at the magazine where I worked. For seven years." Her voice betrayed a touch of bitterness with that last sentence.

"Anyhow," Sarah continued, "we were friends first, but then things...progressed. Got out of hand." She was silent for a moment. She took her glasses off, wiped the steamy lenses with a forefinger to clear them, then put them back on.

"Did you love her?" Dorsey asked. Praying the answer was no.

"No," Sarah said. "I guess I thought I was falling for her, at one point. But...she changed. She got so difficult, so...obsessed. She had to know where I was every minute, when I'd be home, where was I going, who was I talking to. It was crazy. We'd only been together for like six months. I was starting to realize it was a mistake, but I still had feelings for her. And we would still have some good times. But then the magazine was going to send me to Toronto for a week for a story and she completely flipped out. And I mean *flipped out*. Forbade me to go. She was crying, hysterical. It was bad..."

Her voice trailed off for a second, but then she resumed her narrative.

"Anyhow, I knew then I had to break it off and I did. I told her we were through, it was over, got the key to my loft back and went to Toronto. When I got home, all hell had broken loose."

She paused again and looked up at Dorsey. "I guess I should have told you this part up front," Sarah said. "She's the publisher's daughter."

"Oh."

"Yeah, oh. And while I was in Toronto, she was busy taking just enough pills to get her stomach pumped—but not kill her—and making some superficial cuts to one of her wrists that didn't even end up requiring stitches, calling 911 and then artfully collapsing on my bed, because she'd made a copy of the apartment key, unbeknownst to me."

"Jesus," Dorsey said, "that must have been awful."

"Yeah, well, it got worse. As soon as I got back to work, my boss called me into his office, didn't mention Ana at all, but said a bunch of bullshit about me missing a deadline—which wasn't true—and the quality of my work not being up to snuff. Which was also totally not true. Bottom line, they found enough reasons to fire me on the spot."

"God, Sarah," Dorsey said with empathy. Which she sincerely felt, but another part of her was signaling *Drama Alert!* and waving a big yellow caution sign.

Dorsey was not a fan of drama. Other women seemed to thrive on it and even find ways to manufacture it when life didn't provide them with enough, but not her. She liked peace, quiet and harmony. That being said, she did know that drama had a way of sneaking up and hitting you over the head with a frying pan when you least expected it. She hoped this tale of woe of Sarah's was the exception rather than the rule. She was willing to give her the benefit of the doubt so far, but it wouldn't take much more to scare her off, she thought.

"When did all this happen?" Dorsey asked cautiously.

"About three months ago. At first, I couldn't believe it. I mean, fired, after seven years. And for what? Sleeping with daddy's little girl? Shit. Anyhow, I tried finding a job with other magazines, but after a couple of months of polite rejections and people 'forgetting' to return my calls, I got the message—I'm blacklisted. In Chicago, at least."

She looked at Dorsey to see how she was reacting to all this information. "Some sob story, huh?" Sarah tried to say with a smile, but the little catch in her voice gave her away.

Dorsey's arm went around her then, pulling her in close. Sarah pressed her face into Dorsey's shoulder, struggling to regain her composure.

"It sounds like you've been through a lot," Dorsey offered.

"Yeah," Sarah said. She sat up a little straighter, but still leaned into Dorsey's side. Dorsey liked the feeling of her arm around Sarah. It felt like it was meant to be there. The feeling of their slick thighs touching beneath the bubbles wasn't bad, either.

"It was just a mess," Sarah continued. "I finally gave up my apartment, threw all my shit in storage, got in the car and drove straight through to Romeo Falls, just to get away. I knew Maggie would take me in. Guess I kind of forgot about Aunt Viv being part of the package, though," she ended with a wry smile. She took a sip of her beer, then took her glasses off to examine them. They were foggy again from the steam. She set them carefully aside on the deck behind her.

"So what are you going to do?" Dorsey asked her.

"For work, you mean? I've got a few feelers out to people I know in New York and L.A. Financially, at least, I'm not in any rush, thank goodness. I've got enough to see me through the summer. I thought I might use this time in Romeo Falls to finally start work on a novel, actually."

"You're writing a book?" Dorsey was impressed.

"Well, it's just at the notes stage now."

"I always admire people who can write," Dorsey said.

"That's funny, I always admire people who can do things with their hands," Sarah replied.

They shared a small smile. Sarah reached down and picked up Dorsey's hand, measuring her own against it. Even that minimal contact was highly arousing. Dorsey found herself speechless again, overwhelmed by the sensation of Sarah's touch.

Sarah said, "You know, I've thought about you a lot since that night by the lake, Dorsey." With her glasses off, her blue eyes looked even bigger in the moonlight. "Have you...thought about me?" Sarah asked.

Dorsey paused to consider her answer. Frankly, it was kind of hard to reconcile the Sarah right in front of her with the Naked Silver Lake Goddess. She almost seemed like three different people—the cousin she'd heard about and disliked from afar all her life, the Goddess with whom she'd spent just a few magical hours and the real Sarah sitting next to her now in the hot tub. Dorsey knew how she felt about the first two. She wasn't so sure yet about the third.

"Yeah, I've thought about you," she admitted. "And that night. But..."

"But?" Sarah echoed, setting her beer bottle down on the deck and letting go of Dorsey's hand as well, to her disappointment.

"But what about Maggie?" Dorsey said.

Sarah reached over and plucked Dorsey's bottle out of her hand, setting it down on the deck too. She put a hand down on Dorsey's thigh to help her balance as she carefully stood upright in the hot tub, facing Dorsey.

"Maggie who?" she said with a wicked grin as she gracefully slid onto Dorsey's lap, straddling her.

Dorsey felt there was something she should say, but suddenly and completely lost her train of thought as Sarah's firm, wet body took control of all her senses. Sarah's lips met hers with an urgency that Dorsey reveled in. As they kissed, Sarah's hands were running through her hair while Dorsey's hands slid up Sarah's thighs. At her hips, Dorsey's fingers worked their way under the waistband of Sarah's bikini bottoms, pulling them down an inch or two. Sarah gave a small moan as she felt the pressure of Dorsey's hands. She broke their kiss just long enough to rear backward and unsnap her bikini top, which now hung loosely from her neck, the sides of her perfect breasts exposed in the moonlight. As Sarah hurriedly flung her bikini top onto the deck, Dorsey reached for her and pulled her in so she could put her mouth on first one, then the other of her flawless nipples. Sarah gasped and threw her head back as Dorsey sucked and licked, then pushed Dorsey off so she could stand again.

Sarah's breasts swayed in Dorsey's face as she leaned over her, her hands on the deck behind Dorsey's head. Dorsey eased off Sarah's bikini bottoms as Sarah stood challengingly over her, panting with the slowness with which Dorsey was teasing her. Dorsey's face was underwater for a moment as she leaned down to finish guiding the bikini off Sarah's glistening naked body. Sarah restraddled her as she sat back up, kissing her deeply, pressing against her from head to toe. Dorsey tossed the bikini bottoms backward onto the deck, not knowing or caring where they landed as she kissed Sarah back, her mind in joyous tumult that she had her Goddess back again. She couldn't get enough of her—her eyes, her hands, her lips couldn't get enough of her. Her hand slipped in between Sarah's legs. Sarah stiffened for a moment, then adjusted her position to give the hand more room to maneuver. She struggled for breath as Dorsey's fingers slid back and forth.

"Tell me what you want," Dorsey whispered in her ear as Sarah clutched her fiercely. Dorsey kissed her throat as Sarah moved with and against her.

"Just keep—" Sarah managed to gasp, but then both women froze as headlights raked the deck and the house. They heard the gravel crunch as a car turned off the highway onto the long Bartholomew driveway.

"Oh my God," Dorsey groaned as Sarah said, "It's Maggie!"

She leaped off Dorsey's lap and fumbled for her bikini top, which was just behind Dorsey's head on the deck. Dorsey felt overwhelmed with disappointment, but couldn't help but admire the view as a naked Sarah stood above her and yanked her bikini top back on at high speed. Her waist was right at eye level. Dorsey's fingers reached out as if of their own accord to stroke the soft dark strip of hair beneath. Sarah gasped again, then grabbed her hand.

"Stop," she said with a rising note of panic in her voice. She grabbed her glasses from the deck and put them on hurriedly. "Where are my bikini bottoms? Do you see them? She'll be up here any minute..." She swiveled her head around, searching frantically for the missing half of her suit. Dorsey didn't see it either. Thanks to the night, which was now fully dark, and the large potted plants dotting the perimeter of the deck, she felt certain that Maggie hadn't seen anything as she drove up. She could hear the sounds of Maggie parking below, however, so her arrival on the deck was imminent. The car door slammed.

"Just sit down and act casual," she said to Sarah in an undertone. "Here, drink your beer. She won't see anything under the bubbles. I'll see if I can find them."

"Jesus H.," Sarah muttered. But she sat down as Dorsey clambered, dripping, out of the hot tub and Maggie came up the stairs.

"Hey, Mags," they both said more or less normally. Actually,

Dorsey thought that Sarah sounded the more normal of the two of them. What a good actor she is, she thought—and then found the thought oddly unsettling.

"How's Aunt Viv?" Sarah asked.

Dorsey hoped the extra gleam in Sarah's eyes and heightened color in her face would not be as obvious to Maggie as they were to her. With her heart still hammering in her chest, she felt a little overheated herself. As well as dangerously close to a fit of the giggles due to the AWOL bikini bottoms. She stole a quick glance around the deck, but saw no sign of them.

Maggie had headed straight to the table and opened the picnic basket, where she extracted a frosted chocolate cupcake and bit off half of it in one bite. Dorsey brought her a beer to wash it down. While Maggie was thus engaged, Dorsey glanced over at Sarah, who was staring daggers at her from the hot tub. "FIND THEM," she mouthed to Dorsey, who was fighting hard not to laugh while covertly scanning the deck for the missing drawers. While Maggie's back was momentarily turned as she looked for something in the basket, Dorsey shrugged at Sarah, holding her hands up to indicate she didn't see the bikini bottoms anywhere. She resumed her previous pose in a flash as Maggie turned back to them. Sarah feigned interest from the hot tub, while casually glancing at first one, then the next corner of the deck.

"She's fine," Maggie said post-swallow, licking some frosting from the corner of her mouth. "Don't we have any napkins?" She poked around on the table, but didn't find any. "I'll get some paper towels out of the kitchen, if that's okay, Dorse?" she told them, already on her way to the door.

"Good idea," Dorsey said, having just spotted Sarah's bikini bottoms in a large potted succulent off to the side. As Maggie went inside, Dorsey strode over to the succulent and flipped the bottoms to Sarah in one quick movement. She, in turn, put them on under the water, then resumed her casual seated position in the hot tub as Maggie came back out clutching a fistful of paper towels. And helped herself to another cupcake.

"Did y'all not eat yet?" she asked them.

"Uh, no," Dorsey replied. "We were, uh…"

"We thought we'd wait for you, just in case," Sarah said

collectedly. She climbed out of the hot tub and dried herself with the beach towel she'd brought. Dorsey felt a keen pang of disappointment again as she glanced at Sarah, then just as quickly glanced away. Another screwed up chance for the two of them. She dried herself with her T-shirt, then pulled her jeans back on.

"Man, I wish I looked as good in my bathing suit as you two do in yours," Maggie said wistfully as she started on cupcake number three.

"Oh, Maggie, you're fine," her cousin said in what sounded like a tried-and-true refrain. She wound the towel around her waist sarong-style. "But what's up with Aunt Viv? Is her ankle broken or what? What did the doctor say?"

"Well, come sit down and I'll tell you."

They all three sat down at the table as Maggie doled out the food, which was far more than just cupcakes. A cool cucumber salad, home-fried chicken, German potato salad, corn bread and a melon ball medley were just some of the delicacies Maggie had prepared. Her cooking skills were as advanced as her math. Munching away, Dorsey and Sarah listened as Maggie brought them up to speed.

"It's just a sprain, thank goodness. Dr. Melba wrapped it and told her to put it on ice and rest. I got her home and in her bed. She's got it propped up on a bag of frozen peas, is no doubt watching a Lifetime movie as we speak and drinking a glass of wine to go with the Vicodin she found in her medicine cabinet from God knows when. I'm sure the doctor wouldn't approve of that, but you know how Mother is. Hardheaded as all get out. But thank heaven she's all right, more or less."

The other two murmured their assent and they all clinked beer bottles.

"She's already back to her bossy old self," Maggie said with a sigh. "She practically forced me to come back out here. She said I don't get out enough. Anyhow, I should probably get back there pretty soon. I know you're an early riser, Dorse, so I thought I'd come get Sarah so she doesn't keep you up too late. You know how these city girls love to party," she said with a smile at Sarah, who guiltily jumped a little and knocked over her beer.

"Whoops!" she said, blotting up the beer with a corner of her beach towel. Maggie ran to the kitchen to get more paper towels.

Sarah took advantage of her absence to quietly say to Dorsey, "Is it just me, or have you noticed we are constantly getting interrupted?"

"Believe me," Dorsey said grimly, "I've noticed."

They had no more chances that night to talk privately. The three of them finished their dinner, then Maggie and Sarah set off for home. Dorsey watched them drive away, the pang of disappointment now more like a brick in her chest. The memories of Sarah's wet skin, of her mouth on Sarah's breasts and Sarah's hands in her hair were tantalizingly painful. Just another missed opportunity, she thought. Another disaster.

George the big gray cat slunk grumpily down the alleyway behind the hardware store. Ira skittered manically along behind him, leaping at night insects flying well out of his range overhead, pouncing on shadows, bouncing off the brick walls of the buildings in his usual hyper fashion. They were headed for the trash bin behind the Sizzle'N'Shake. There was always something good in or around it. Plus, there was a streetlight nearby. George liked to sit at its base and ponder the moths fluttering in its bright beam while Ira danced around, throwing punches in the air. And eventually succumbing to his pathological need to swat the tip of George's restless tail, which always ended with the big gray kicking his much smaller tabby ass, but he still never could resist.

George paused and crouched down as they reached the mouth of the alley. His luminous green eyes narrowed to slits. Ira skidded to a stop as well, nearly running into George's generous hindquarters as the night breeze brought a scent of something slightly unusual on their midnight excursions. A human. The acrid smell of stress sweat announced the person to the cats like a blare of trumpets. There was another smell as well, one they recognized from their hardware store—the chemical smell of paint.

Footsteps approached the alley.

"Here, kitty, kitty," a hoarse voice whispered. George flattened his ears back and hissed, but stood his ground. Ira, more easily spooked, backed off into the shadows, then leaped lightly up to the top of a Dumpster. He felt safer in the darkness there, plus he had a bird's-eye view of whatever was going down. George was pissed, he could tell, but then George was almost always pissed. And something was wrong with this picture...

George's tail lashed the ground as the human bent down to pick him up.

"That's a good kitty," said the whisperer, whose hands gripped George tighter and tighter. He struggled to free himself, slashing a jacket sleeve and then the flesh beneath with his razor claws which earned a guttural "Son of a bitch!" from his captor, but still the hands held him in a steely, vise-like grip.

"Gotcha, you little bastard," said the voice triumphantly. The person stood up as George yowled and writhed to no avail. Until Ira launched himself from the top of the Dumpster onto the attacker's head. The human shrieked and twirled, dropping George to flail blindly at Ira, who leaped off as soon as George was clear. The two cats raced away at high speed with George in the lead. The big smoky gray was unhurt, as was Ira, who had a little extra swagger in his scamper. No sweaty, crazed human was going to hurt his George—Super Ira to the rescue!

CHAPTER FIVE

Luke had a feeling the decapitated carnations would not be the end of it. First, the town's highway sign. Then, Mrs. Gargoyle's flowers. (In his mind, he still called her that, although he was scrupulous about always referring to her as Officer Argyle out loud, even to his wife.) Someone was just getting warmed up, Luke knew. In a sense, he had been waiting for the call that came from Pastor Reinhardt early Thursday morning. In the grassy area in front of the Presbyterian church, a small sign announced the title of each week's sermon for the faithful, spelled out in white plastic letters on a black background. A lockable glass door kept the letters safe from the weather.

Luke and Mrs. Gargoyle stood with the pastor in front of his vandalized sign. The little white plastic letters that had previously spelled out "Eternity Is No Summer Vacation: Are

Your Bags Packed For Heaven Or Hell?" now lay strewn about in the grass. Larger and more colorful plastic letters had taken their place:

U SUCK
KTHNXBAI

A slash of red spray paint underlined the colorful plastic letters, which Luke recognized. They looked like the alphabet and number magnets adorning his refrigerator door at home. The older of his two little girls liked to spell out words with them.

"I get the 'u suck' part of it," the pastor said heavily. "But what does the rest of it mean, Luke?"

"It's an expression people use when they're texting on a cell phone," Luke told him. "It's short for 'okay, thanks, bye'—but in a sarcastic, dismissive kind of way. Like if someone tells you something you already know. You know what I mean?"

Pastor Reinhardt nodded, but he looked even more disturbed than before. "So you think it was a kid then?" he asked the two police officers.

"I wouldn't jump to that conclusion," Luke said. "Lots of people text these days, not just kids."

Without touching the sign, he studied the glass door. It was unbroken. It had probably been jimmied open, with a jackknife blade or a nail file in its simple lock. Luke glanced more closely at the door—there was a small smear of what looked like blood on the frame. It looked fresh.

"You see that?" he said to Gargoyle, pointing it out with his pen but making sure not to touch it. She nodded.

"I'll get the camera and the evidence kit," she said.

"Maybe we'll get lucky and there will be fingerprints this time," Luke said. The shoebox and its wrapping paper had been devoid of prints or any other clues.

Pastor Reinhardt had a sour expression on his face, which deepened at the mention of fingerprints.

"Luke, you know my prints will be on there," he said.

"Of course, sir," Luke replied. "Whose else should we expect to find?"

"Sometimes my wife puts the letters up," the pastor replied, still sounding disheartened. "And...sometimes my daughter."

"So, you're telling me Mariah's prints will likely be on there," Luke said, careful to make it a neutral statement, not a question or an accusation.

"Yes."

"Was that blood there before?" Luke asked him.

"Not to my knowledge," said the pastor. "And I'm the one who changed the letters this week." His eyes looked despairing. "You don't think she did it, do you, Luke? Surely she wouldn't go so far as to attack our church...to attack me like this..."

"I don't know who did this, Pastor," Luke told him. "And I don't know why, or if this is the end of it. But I'm going to find out all those things." There was an edge to his voice as he finished his statement.

"Whoever did this needs our understanding, Luke. Understanding and forgiveness," Pastor Reinhardt said. His eyes looked worried now, his brow deeply furrowed.

"That's your end of it, Padre," Luke said, although not without compassion. "I just catch 'em."

CHAPTER SIX

Dorsey was having a late breakfast at the Blue Duck's counter when the chief of police came in and sat down next to her.

"Mornin', Luke," she said.

"Dorsey."

He ordered coffee and a cinnamon roll to go while she went back to her scrambled eggs and bacon. The rest of the stools at the counter were empty, so he obviously had something to say to her. She hoped it wasn't a continuation of his lecture from the other night. She liked Luke, but she certainly didn't need his advice on her love life. Or lack thereof.

The weather had turned cool and rainy again, with more thundershowers forecast for the afternoon and evening. It was her day off from the hardware store and since working outside on the Bartholomews' deck was not an option, her plan was to run some errands, go for a swim and then work in the woodshop. She had gone home the night before after the latest miscue with Sarah feeling both depressed and restless. Depressed because what the hell was she thinking, fooling around with Maggie's cousin behind her back? There was no way that was going to end well and she should know better. She did know better. She should either break it off completely with Sarah or get her to come clean with Maggie. But what was the point anyhow, she thought morosely. Sarah would no doubt get sick of small-town life in another week or two and take off, leaving Dorsey behind to deal with the inevitable damage to both her heart and her friendship with Mags.

The restlessness was more on a physical level. She knew she wouldn't sleep when she got home, so she'd worked in the woodshop until long past midnight. Her current project was a dining room table and chairs. She sometimes built original items from scratch, but her favorite thing was to find an old piece of furniture—a chair, a table, a chest of drawers—at a garage sale, at the curb on trash day, or occasionally at the swap meet in Grover and "re-imagine" it. She would not just restore it, but completely re-do it, incorporating different kinds of wood to add color and texture and using different bits from different pieces of old furniture to give whatever she was working on a truly unique and original look. Her imagination and her father's training were her only guides. The former added the style while the latter ensured the function. Some of her "experiments" turned out better than others, but all were high quality, one-of-a-kind pieces. The Larue house was full of her more successful works. She'd given Maggie a few pieces as well. Goodman let her show some pieces in the front display window of the hardware store, but she hadn't had much luck selling them so far. Still, her hobby was a great source of comfort to her. It felt good just being in the workshop that her father had built, smelling the familiar scents of wood, linseed oil and turpentine. Using the tools and knowledge he had endowed her with made her feel useful and loved, at least for a few hours at a time.

Luke's mother-in-law brought him his coffee and roll. Despite the cool turn to the weather, he was in shirtsleeves, his tan uniform looking crisp and wrinkle-free. There were a few other late morning diners at the tables, but no one within earshot of their seats at the counter. The restaurant was peaceful and quiet in the lull between the morning rush and lunch hour.

Luke surprised her by saying, "I suppose you heard about the Presbyterian church's sign."

"Uh, yeah, I have," she said. "People were talking about it when I came in here this morning. I guess somebody's got it in for the signs around town, huh?"

"It's not just signs, Dorsey. You may have heard about Officer Argyle's flowers as well."

She nodded, but knowing how little affection many of Mrs. Gargoyle's former students felt for the one-time junior high school teacher, Dorsey wondered if that particular incident was really part of the same pattern. She didn't want to say as much to Luke's face, however, since he had to work with the woman. Besides, she really didn't care. A couple of signs and some carnations were messed up—some crime wave, she thought.

Sensing her lack of interest, Luke said, "You may not have heard this part, Dorse. Somebody spray-painted the flower heads and mailed them to the police station. And the church sign was spray-painted, as well."

Dorsey nodded while chewing the last mouthful of her eggs. BFD, she thought. Luke clearly didn't have enough real crime to keep him busy. Thank goodness. He was looking at her, though, as if some response was required on her part. She swallowed and said, "So, what, you think it's some kid?"

"I don't know, Dorsey," he said seriously, his eyes pinned on hers. "I see a pattern of someone disrespecting our town, our police force and a church, though. And that's just the pattern up to now. I don't think he—or she—is done yet."

His last sentence was said with some emphasis. So far, Dorsey had no idea why he was telling her all this. Luke didn't usually bother to discuss crime-solving or anything else with her. Their paths didn't cross that often these days since he wasn't hanging out with Good so much.

"Well, I'm sure if you round up the usual suspects, you'll figure it out in no time, Luke," she said encouragingly, hoping to wrap up their little chat so she could go run her errands. She looked around for the waitress and signaled for the check. He reclaimed her attention with a hand on her arm.

"That's just it, Dorse—I don't know if the usual suspects will cover it in this case," he told her.

She looked at him, confused. And then the light dawned. She cocked her head and said to him in a fierce undertone, "Oh my God, are you saying you think *Sarah* has something to do with all this?"

"I don't know," he said. "My investigation is ongoing."

"But that's what you're trying to suggest to me—that she could be the perpetrator?"

"All I'm suggesting," Luke said with another meaningful look at her, "is that you be careful. Someone out there has got it in for this town. For all of us, maybe. And I don't know if he or she is going to be satisfied with just vandalism."

"But why?" Dorsey was bewildered. "Why in the world would Sarah deface the highway sign, for starters?"

"I heard she had some less-than-positive things to say about small towns the other night at The Hamlet," Luke answered. "And you know how city people always think we're just a bunch of dumb hicks out here."

"That's pretty fucking weak, Luke," Dorsey said, incensed.

"Watch your language," he said mildly, one eye on his mother-in-law who was making a fresh pot of coffee down at the other end of the counter.

"Well, what about the f-...reakin' carnations?"

"Officer Argyle gave her a ticket her first night in town," he reminded her.

"Look, this is ridiculous!" Dorsey burst out. "I can't believe you're even thinking this. What's your explanation for the church sign then?"

"I don't know about that one," Luke admitted. "Yet," he added significantly.

Meanwhile, Sarah's words from the night before about not being able to stand religious people had come floating back into Dorsey's brain. But Sarah had been with her and Maggie last night, her brain fought back.

"When was the church sign vandalized?" she asked Luke.

"After one a.m.," he said. "I drove past it myself at one and it was fine then. I remember chuckling at the pastor's sermon title. And I definitely would have noticed the more colorful version."

Sarah and Maggie had left the Bartholomew farm before ten o'clock, Dorsey knew. Plenty of time, a voice in her brain said... She shook her head, as much to ward off the unwelcome thought as to express her disagreement with Luke.

"I still think this is crazy," she told him. "Do you seriously think Sarah could have done any of this?"

"I don't know," he repeated. "But I know she's a stranger here. And maybe you should...exercise a little caution. You know what I mean, Dorse?"

She looked at him, unable to decide whether she was more irritated or confused.

"You don't even know her, Luke," she finally said.

"You're right. I don't. And neither do you. Just take it slow, Dorsey, is all I'm saying. Be careful."

"I know her a lot better than you do," she shot back. "And she's Maggie's cousin, for crying out loud!"

"Look, Dorsey, I'm not at liberty to discuss every aspect of this case with you, all right? But I've talked to some people in Chicago and your new friend Sarah may not be as perfect as you think she is."

"I never said she was perfect," Dorsey said defensively. She thought back over the things Sarah had told her. About her crazy ex-girlfriend... and getting fired... and getting her prescription filled at the pharmacy...

"Is this about her break-up with that co-worker she was dating?" She very nearly said "her girlfriend" before remembering not to out Sarah to Luke, although she thought he'd probably figured that part out for himself already. Or maybe he had more than just suspicions—who knew what the cops in Chicago or whoever he had talked with had told him? There were more than a few Romeo Falls natives now residing in the Windy City, so he might have reached out to that grapevine as well.

"Dorsey, all I'm saying is be careful, okay?" Luke's tone

was patient and kind. "She's a stranger and sometimes...well, sometimes, strangers are trouble. Just watch yourself, okay, kiddo?"

Dorsey shook her head, still trying to deny everything he was saying. Trying to ignore the suspicions he was raising in her. And ignore the voice in her head that kept bringing up things Sarah had said.

But—not Sarah! It couldn't be Sarah... could it?

She looked back at Luke. He looked tired and concerned. Some of that concern was for her, she knew, but she still couldn't wrap her mind around it. She shook her head again as he stood.

"Breakfast doesn't cause lunch, Luke."

He involuntarily glanced at the remains of her own breakfast on the counter.

"Meaning?"

"Just because there's someone new in town doesn't mean she's the one behind all of this."

"And yet nothing was happening before she got here."

Dorsey sat there, staring up at him, unable to think of any reply. He picked up his coffee and cinnamon roll and left her there to contemplate that one undeniable fact.

She thought about Luke's warning as she ran her errands. It bothered her more than she wanted to admit that he was even considering Sarah as a possible suspect. His evidence, if you could even call it that, was circumstantial at best, she thought. In the end, she had to go with her gut—and her gut said Sarah was a good person. A good person she needed to set some boundaries with pronto. She decided she would call Maggie's house when she got home, see if she could talk to Sarah then and clear the whole matter up.

She felt better after reaching that resolution. Having visited the bank and the drugstore already that morning, she was about to turn her little pickup truck in the direction of the community center so she could do her laps in the pool. As she turned down Main, though, she remembered she wanted to pick up some sandpaper at the hardware store. A spot was open right in front of the store—right next to a cherry red Bug, as it turned out.

The bell gave its familiar jangle as she entered the store. She nodded to Shaw, who was half asleep behind the register. Duke Ellington was playing quietly in the background as she looked around for Sarah. Why would she be here? Was she looking for Dorsey? Dorsey realized her heart was racing. She told herself sternly to calm down and act like a civilized, reasonable adult—her only purpose in seeing Sarah was to cool things down between them. She told herself that, but her heart was still racing. She could hear Goodman talking to a customer around the corner, but couldn't see who that was. Laughter in response to something Good said made her pulse jump up a notch—she recognized the voices of both Sarah and Maggie.

She found herself heading down the paint aisle, ostensibly to get the sandpaper, but in reality to buy a little time before she had to speak to them. Since she had no idea what she was going to say, a little preparation seemed in order. Before she could assemble her scattered wits, though, all three of them came around the far corner of the aisle and headed her way.

"Well, Dorsey, there you are," Maggie said happily, walking toward her. "I called the house but nobody was home."

Goodman was behind Maggie, hovering over her like a benevolent grizzly. Sarah had stopped short in the aisle behind him when she caught sight of Dorsey. She and Dorsey exchanged a quick glance. It was like opening the oven door and getting that quick blast of heat, Dorsey thought. The mere fact of Sarah's presence set her aflame. All her well-intentioned thoughts of breaking it off were blown away like thistle down on a hot summer wind. With an effort, she jerked her attention back to Maggie and Goodman. Good was focused on Maggie, the customer, but Maggie herself was looking rather oddly at Dorsey.

"Dorse? Are you all right?"

"Yeah, of course," Dorsey said with a shrug and moved forward to join Maggie and Goodman where they had stopped. She realized they were back in front of the spray paint display.

"Royal blue, you said?" Good asked Maggie. He unlocked the cabinet and selected a can. "How about this?"

"Perfect," Maggie said, beaming up at Good. He smiled back at her.

"We decided to go with blue instead of red for the chairs," Maggie explained to Dorsey.

"Hmm? Oh. Great," she said, trying to pay attention to Maggie while her entire body was focused on Sarah. She snuck a peek at her. The city girl was still hanging back about ten feet down the aisle, engrossed in a text message on her cell phone. She was looking good, if a bit somber, in a charcoal gray long-sleeved Henley shirt and black jeans. Dorsey loved the way her pale, slender neck looked emerging from the dark shirt. She longed to touch Sarah's soft black spiky hair, to feel her warm body pressed up against her, just one more time...

Goodman said jokingly to her, "You didn't forget it's your day off, right?"

"Oh. No. Just needed some sandpaper."

"Well, take what you need," he said generously.

He was showing off for Maggie and Sarah, Dorsey thought wryly. Normally, he would make her pay the wholesale price for it, but she was not above taking advantage of his momentary fiscal lapse. She selected a pack from the shelf opposite and put it in her backpack. Good, his arms full of blue paint cans, was shepherding Maggie past her toward the front counter. Sarah, still concentrating on her texting, drifted along behind. Dorsey walked with her to the front display window as Good took Maggie off to the register. There was an awkward ten foot square of empty space by the display window, remnant of an earlier renovation done by the Larues' grandfather. He'd knocked down one wall, then put up another. Good mostly left the space empty these days—if nothing else, it made loading and unloading the front display window easier.

Sarah snapped her phone closed and stuck it in her jeans pocket. "Sorry," she said to Dorsey. "Just catching up with a friend in L.A."

Dorsey felt obscurely jealous, then realized how ridiculous that was. She nodded, at a loss for words now that they were face to face and alone for the moment. Just for something to do, she reached into the display window and made a miniscule adjustment to the rocking chair that was set up in there, next to a chest of drawers. Both were her work. A selection of household items was displayed on and around the furniture, reflecting the current sale. George the cat (not for sale) lazed in the rocker, enjoying the shaft of late morning sunlight that warmed the front window. He narrowed his eyes at Dorsey when she moved the chair slightly, then huffily jumped down and stalked off to a different spot.

Sarah laughed at his reaction. "What a diva he is!" she said to Dorsey.

Ira had been lurking in one of the half-open drawers of the dresser, which featured a beguiling display of smoke detectors and nine volt batteries. His head popped out when he heard George thump to the floor. He watched as the larger cat slowly walked the length of the display window, rubbing his side against the foot high back wall. Sensing that George's mood was even fouler than usual, Ira prudently returned to the depths of the drawer. The big gray came to a stop in front of where Sarah was standing and stared up at her malevolently.

"I wouldn't try to pet him," Dorsey warned in case Sarah was considering it. "He might let you pick him up, but then he'd just scratch the shit out of you. He's done it to me more than once."

"And he's your cat!" Sarah exclaimed.

"Oh, no. The cats are Goodman's. They were his idea—you know, small town, cute kitties in the hardware store window? He thought they would add flavor or atmosphere or something. Local color. Like the swing music playing all the time."

"You don't like them?" Sarah asked.

Dorsey shrugged. "His store, his cats. Doesn't make any difference to me. It's funny, though—the only person besides Good that George tolerates is Maggie, believe it or not."

"Oh, well, everybody loves Maggie," said Sarah, as if stating the obvious. "And trust me—I have no intention of petting him. I've already suffered one animal attack this week and that was more than enough."

She pulled up the sleeve of her shirt to show Dorsey a raw-looking scratch on her pale forearm. "That damn Carmichael," she explained. "We should have had the vet clip his nails when he had him the other night. He was chewing on the remote under the sofa the other day and I made the mistake of trying to retrieve it. The little shit."

"Ouch," said Dorsey, sympathetically.

Sarah glanced back in the display window. "You know, I love that dresser—there's one kind of like it in my room at Maggie's."

"I know," Dorsey replied. "I made it."

"What? For real? You made those beautiful dressers?" Sarah exclaimed. She sounded more impressed than disbelieving.

"Well, I guess 'rebuilt' would be a better word."

Dorsey gestured toward a small hand-lettered card in the corner of the display window: *Re-imagined Furniture by Dorsey Larue.*

Sarah said, "Wow. I mean, I knew you were a carpenter, but this—this is amazing, Dorsey. Amazing and beautiful. You are really talented."

Dorsey felt a little embarrassed by this unexpected onslaught of compliments. But also extremely pleased that this woman she found so attractive, so compelling—so goddamn hot—liked her furniture, which was really just an extension of her. The two of them exchanged a long, wordless look which was charged with possibility. A small part of Dorsey's mind tried to remind her this was exactly the road she had vowed not to go down again. Confused by her mixture of feelings, she broke off the look and stared blindly out the front window. Thankfully, Maggie had completed her transaction and was coming back to them with a bag full of clanking paint cans, followed by Good. Luke's warning suddenly resurfaced in Dorsey's mind, bringing a question to mind with it.

"Did you return the red paint?" she asked Maggie curiously.

"No, I'm sure I'll use it for something eventually," Maggie said. She was an avid arts-and-crafter. "Now, what are you up to this afternoon? Do you want to go shopping with us in Grover? We're going to the new mall over there."

Shopping had never interested Dorsey, much to Maggie's dismay, who considered it a higher calling. She never gave up hope, though, that her friend might magically transform into a fashionista one day.

"No, thanks, Mags, I'm going swimming."

"Oh, sure, be healthy," Maggie said, kidding. She sighed. "I know I should exercise more like you two do."

"You look fine, Maggie."

Dorsey had been expecting Sarah to say the words but, surprisingly, they came from Goodman. All three of the women turned to look up at him as he made this unexpected contribution to the conversation. Maggie blushed becomingly.

Goodman had flushed a little himself, but stuck to his guns. "Well, I mean it," he said somewhat defensively. "I think a woman looks good with a little flesh on her bones...I mean, uh...er..." Goodman suddenly seemed to recall an urgent task awaiting him down aisle two (Electrical/Lighting) and walked off without another word.

Maggie looked shocked, but pleased. Sarah, laughing, squeezed her arm and said, "I think someone's got an admirer, Mags."

Dorsey thought her older brother must be losing his mind—first, the free sandpaper, now this. She looked over at Shaw behind the register to see what his reaction was, if any. He was on his feet, looking out toward Main through the window. Dorsey turned to see what had caught his eye. Dr. Melba Porter was out there, examining the contents of their display window like an anthropologist studying the relics of a lost tribe of the Amazon. Feeling Dorsey's gaze on her, she looked up, saw the three of them standing there and seemed to make up her mind to come in.

Dorsey had met the woman, of course, but hadn't really gotten to know her in the six months or so since she'd come to town. She got what little medical care she needed in Grover because the previous town doctor in Romeo Falls had been a homophobic old asshole who kept trying to cure her of her gayness via pamphlets and various Dire Warnings. Shaw too, got his allergy shots in Grover since the same irascible practitioner had refused to see him anymore after Shaw broke up with his granddaughter in high school.

Dr. Melba was sort of attractive, in a sturdy, intense, humorless kind of way. In her early thirties, she was dark-haired, robust and serious in both her demeanor and attire. Dorsey had seen her 'power-walking' along the side of the highway in all kinds of weather, another big-city predilection that only emphasized her outsider status to the natives. Her inability to make small talk (or dislike of its inefficiency) was not winning over her new neighbors, but since she was the only doctor in town, her practice had a more or less captive audience. Dorsey suspected she might just be shy, an unforgivable sin in Romeo Falls. Maggie, who was her patient and who could always be counted on to see the good in people, said she seemed very smart. Dorsey had not always found that to be a given with doctors, but took Maggie's word for it. Perhaps, she thought, Dr. Melba was one of those people who are so smart that they're tongue-tied with all the information crowding their brains, forever finding themselves three or four steps ahead of the rest of us and doomed to eternally wait for those who will never catch up.

The bell did its thing as she came in. The good doctor headed straight for Maggie. "How's your mother, Mary Margaret?" she said peremptorily.

"She's fine, Doctor. Resting at home. Thank you again for all your help last night," Maggie told her.

Having settled that, the doctor nodded brusquely and then turned to Dorsey. "How much for the rocking chair?" she asked.

"Oh, um, gosh—I don't know," Dorsey said, completely surprised. She had sold so little of the furniture she had given up expecting anyone to take an interest. She didn't even bother to put price tags on her pieces. Goodman was really just indulging her by letting her put a few things in the window. Besides, he had to stack the smoke detectors on something.

"It's for sale, isn't it?" Melba persisted.

"Well, yeah—" Dorsey started, but the doctor interrupted when her answer was too slow in coming.

"What's the price then?" she said, somewhere on the scale between eager and impatient. "You made it, right?"

"Yeah, but it's just a hobby," Dorsey tried to explain.

"Just a hobby?" Dr. Melba was fired up. "Are you kidding me? People in Chicago would go crazy for this stuff. I've got a friend who runs a design store there. This is exactly the kind of unique piece she's always looking for. Do you mind if I send her a picture?" Melba was already whipping out her cell phone.

"Well, okay, sure," Dorsey said, a bit taken aback by the speed at which the doctor was moving. Melba was aiming her phone and taking shots of both the rocker and the dresser. Dorsey looked over at Maggie blankly. Her best friend was beaming, clearly thrilled by this recognition of Dorsey's talent which she'd always loyally supported.

Sarah said inquiringly, "Haven't you sold your stuff before? I mean, it's wonderful—I would think people would be flocking to buy it."

Dorsey snorted. "Not in this town."

"Why not?" Sarah asked.

Dorsey gave her a look that spoke volumes, but just a one-word answer. "Cooties."

"Oh, come on!" Maggie protested, always ready to defend her beloved hometown.

Over the years, she had seen how the town treated Dorsey with her own eyes, of course, but Maggie always found some excuse, some reason to explain away what Dorsey knew to be homophobia, pure and simple. It was important to Mags to see the good in people—even when it wasn't always there, Dorsey thought. She loved Maggie with all her heart and cherished their friendship, but that didn't stop her from sometimes wanting to rip off those rose-colored spectacles her friend was so fond of.

"Remember?" Maggie was saying to her. "You sold that beautiful armoire to the Sizzle Sisters last fall, right?"

"That's true," Dorsey admitted. "And a rolltop desk to a couple in a Winnebago passing through from Wichita. And I've given Maggie a few pieces over the years."

"She won't let me buy any," Maggie pouted to Sarah.

"And that's it," Dorsey said, ignoring Maggie. "It's not to everyone's taste, I guess. Especially around here."

"Well, I like it," said Sarah firmly. "A lot."

"So do I," pronounced the doctor, having finished her photo

shoot. Her phone buzzed at her. She checked the screen. "And so does my friend in Chicago! She wants me to get your business card for her."

Dorsey laughed. "I don't have a business card, but you're welcome to give her the hardware store's number if you like."

"Don't laugh," Melba admonished, brandishing her phone emphatically. "If she likes your stuff enough to buy it, this could be very lucrative for you."

Dorsey shook her head wonderingly, not believing a word of it. Still, it was nice to hear. Maggie looked like she was about to bust her buttons, like she'd invented Dorsey herself. Even Shaw was sidling over, curious as to what all the commotion was about.

Sarah said, "Cool phone, Dr. Porter—is that the new one?"

The two of them compared technologies for a moment.

Dr. Melba said, "I was worried about the service when I first moved here, but the signal's very strong here in town. Now if we could just get Wi-Fi!"

The two urbanites laughed a little about that. "And a decent cup of coffee," Dr. Melba added.

"We've got some nice coffee machines in stock, Doctor, if you're in the market for one of those," Dorsey said.

"It might come to that," Dr. Melba replied, "but when it comes to fancy coffee, it's so nice to have someone else make it for you. You know, somewhere where I could sit down with my laptop, do a little work, check my e-mail and sip my coffee. That's one thing I miss about Chicago."

They all thought about that for a moment, Sarah nodding in agreement and Maggie apparently in fierce concentration.

"You know," Mags said slowly, "it wouldn't be hard at all to set up Wi-Fi in here."

"In here? In the hardware store?" Dorsey asked her, in astonishment. "What on earth for?"

"To bring in more customers, of course," Maggie said with a smile. "I am an MBA, remember?"

"But how would that work?"

"Well, you've got this empty space here. You could set up some chairs and tables—I know you've got plenty of those,

Dorsey," Maggie said wryly. "If you had a Wi-Fi hub, people could bring in their laptops and take advantage of that. And once you've got them in the store, you've got a chance to make a sale, right?"

"Well, yeah, I guess," Dorsey said, still skeptical. "But aside from Dr. Porter here and some of the other tech-savvy young adults, wouldn't that draw in mostly teenagers?"

"Teenagers with disposable cash," Maggie said persuasively. "And it won't be long before the rest of Romeo Falls joins the twenty-first century and has their smart phones and tablets, as well. Trust me—I see it happening with the next generation already. You and Goodman could really get a jump on things if y'all were the first to offer Wi-Fi in town."

"I don't know, Mags," Dorsey said dubiously. "I don't think Good will want to deal with a bunch of unruly teenagers. I mean, who's going to keep them in line?"

"Well, I could," Maggie said. "I mean, obviously, I'm a high school teacher, so I could. But my point is, it's a learnable skill, like anything else. Like lion-taming, as we say in the teacher's lounge!"

They all chuckled at that image.

"And if you could sell some good coffee too," Dr. Melba said plaintively.

"Whoa!" Dorsey laughed. "We're getting kind of far afield from hardware here. First Wi-Fi and now mocha lattes!"

"Well, think about it," Maggie said. She was in her persuasive MBA mode again, her brain clearly calculating all the potential profit to be made. "You could make the coffee free at first to draw them in, then you charge a reasonable price per cup after that. You could use one of the machines you already have in stock. And you could give them a card entitling them to free Wi-Fi for a year if they make a big-ticket purchase—like a single item over three hundred dollars, or five hundred or whatever. That way, the teenagers pester their parents into buying that big-ticket item here, instead of in Grover. You know, most people hate making that drive into GC anyway, especially when it's raining or snowing. Give them an excuse to buy here and they might just do it." Maggie looked dreamy-eyed with possibility.

Sarah chimed in, "That sounds pretty brilliant to me, Mags. If I lived here, I'd be wanting my Wi-Fi card and coffee."

"Me too," said Dr. Melba firmly. "Sign me up."

They all turned and looked at Dorsey expectantly, who held up her hands in surrender. "Sounds brilliant to me too, Mags, but I just work here, you know. You should run it past Good, though. You can explain it a lot better than I can."

Maggie smiled with satisfaction. "I might just do that."

Dr. Melba said to Dorsey, "Now about that rocking chair—is it an antique, by the way?"

"I guess you could call it that."

She didn't want to tell her she'd rescued it from the county dump. They settled on a price that seemed to please Dr. Melba. It certainly pleased Dorsey—it would buy her groceries for the next month.

"I'm on foot here," the doctor told her. "Can your staff deliver this to my home?"

The "staff," in the form of Shaw, cheerfully assured her he could. Since her house was only about a quarter of a mile away, just a block off the town square, Shaw left with her a few minutes later, toting the chair upside down on his head. They seemed to be chatting easily as they walked off down Main, although heaven only knew about what.

"Well," Maggie exclaimed with satisfaction. "Wasn't that just *great*!" She smiled happily at all of them—Dorsey, Sarah and Good, who had resurfaced to man the register in Shaw's absence—impartially. They all smiled back. Maggie's enthusiasm was always infectious. She reached down into the display window to pick up George, who actually started purring as she cuddled him.

"Unbelievable," Sarah said into Dorsey's ear. She turned her head to find the city girl mere inches away. They exchanged a long look as Maggie took George over to his owner, saying "Gosh almighty, Goodman, what are you feeding this creature? I think he's gained more weight this year than I have." Having Sarah so close to her was both exciting and uncomfortable at the same time. She thought it prudent to put some distance between the two of them, walking as casually as she could over to the counter where she set her backpack down and fiddled with it, so she wouldn't have to make eye contact with any of them.

"Ready to go, Sarah?" Maggie said.

"Oh, um, actually, is it okay if I use the restroom?"

Good hated it when Dorsey let customers use the tiny employee bathroom, except (maybe) for Maggie who got the "best friend" pass. But his uncharacteristic behavior was still in effect, apparently.

"Of course," he told Sarah graciously. "Dorsey, do you want to show her where it is?"

So Sarah followed Dorsey behind the counter, through the doorway and down the hall toward the little restroom. Behind them, they heard Maggie telling Goodman about her Wi-Fi idea.

"It's right here," Dorsey said to Sarah, indicating the open door of the restroom.

"What's this? The office?" Sarah said, stopping short at another opening. She peered in with interest.

"Yeah, that's the office," Dorsey said, walking back to her side. Whereupon Sarah grabbed her hand, pulled her into the office and pressed her up against the wall for a long, intense, no-holds-barred kiss.

All of Dorsey's good intentions melted away. It felt so good— so right—kissing Sarah. There was a couch in the small office, covered as always with piles of paperwork. Somehow she found herself on that couch, underneath Sarah, papers slithering and crackling underneath, urgent lips locked together and her hands on Sarah's back underneath her shirt.

"I was thinking about you all night," Sarah murmured as she kissed Dorsey's neck, her hands on Dorsey's breasts. Time was passing all too quickly. Dorsey pulled Sarah back up to taste her lips once again.

They heard Goodman's voice from the far end of the hall.

"Dorse?" he called inquiringly. She pulled out of another brain-melting kiss just long enough to call back a semi-strangled "We'll be right there, Good." During that brief moment Sarah managed to get the top button of Dorsey's jeans undone and the zipper halfway down.

"Stop," she hissed at Sarah while her brother answered with an "Okay." Sarah hooked the tip of her index finger under the waistband of Dorsey's panties and fixed her with a penetrating gaze.

"Stop?" she whispered. They both were breathing heavily.

"We have to stop," Dorsey gasped. "This has to stop. They're right out there, for God's sake."

Did she want to get caught, Dorsey wondered. Sarah seemed to consider her words for a moment, then sighed. She leaned in to trace Dorsey's lower lip with the tip of her tongue, then kissed her softly and quickly one last time.

"Fine," she said and reluctantly peeled herself off Dorsey. She pulled Dorsey to her feet, where she just naturally seemed to fit into Sarah's arms.

"Don't you have to pee?" Dorsey asked, her hands not missing the opportunity to cup Sarah's tight ass.

"Nah, that was just an excuse to get you alone and put my hand down your pants."

"Your hand's not down—oh, oh my God...no, stop, Sarah. Stop."

Dorsey was halfway laughing and all the way turned on, but she had to make Sarah stop. Getting caught was not an option. Even if that was what Sarah consciously or subconsciously wanted, Dorsey could think of several less embarrassing ways to break the news to Maggie. She determinedly pulled away and got her jeans zipped up.

She ran her hands through her hair and hoped it wasn't looking too crazy. Sarah, smiling to herself, stepped into the restroom to check hers in the mirror. Dorsey would have liked to go in there and splash some cold water on her face, but she didn't dare delay any longer. She quickly straightened out the papers on the couch, then did several deep inhales, trying to regain her composure.

She followed a still grinning Sarah down the hall back into the store where Maggie and Good awaited them. The four of them said their goodbyes, then the other two women left in Sarah's VW, while Dorsey drove slowly to the community center.

Remembering all the while that she had meant to break it off with Sarah. End it before things got messy. Before she got hurt. Or Maggie... Instead, things seemed to be escalating at a dizzying pace.

She could still feel Sarah's lips on hers. Feel Sarah's hands on her skin—and her hands on Sarah's. At a red light, she looked at herself in her rearview mirror. Her reflection bit its lip and looked confused.

With the kids out of school, the indoor pool at the community center was pretty packed, but luckily they had a few lanes roped off for adult lap swimmers. Dorsey tuned out the noise and the other people and concentrated on getting into the Zen of her mile-long swim. Afterward, feeling tired but contented from the workout, she pulled herself from the pool and headed for the women's locker room to change back into street clothes. She would shower at home, as usual. Showering in the locker room was simply too tiresome. The reaction to her even using a locker in there had ranged from a glacial chill to "righteous" outrage. The last time she'd attempted a shower, a young mother who'd been a year behind her in school had actually clapped her hands over the eyes of her six-year-old daughter when Dorsey had stepped out, modestly wrapped in a beach towel. Apparently, even just seeing a lesbian in the locker room was enough to scar the child forever.

Well, she told herself, they might have run her out of the showers, but she would not let them run her out of the pool. Goddammit, she was as much a part of this town as they were. Larue's Swingtime Hardware had helped raise the money that had built the community center and had contributed some of the building materials.

As usual, when she entered the locker room, all conversation stopped for a second, then resumed. At the end of her row of lockers, three young girls were chattering like birds—Wild Child

Mariah, the preacher's daughter, and two of her high school buddies, Jimalene White the reigning Fair Queen (daughter of proud parents Jim and—you guessed it—Alene White) and Kelly Blankenship, the bank manager's daughter.

"I know," she heard Mariah say to the other two, apparently picking up where their conversation had left off. "My dad's an asshole like that too. He made me do a bunch of yard work this morning, can you believe it? Check this out—I scratched the shit out of my arm picking up brush in the backyard."

Dorsey ignored them as she finished toweling off, then threw on her jeans and T-shirt over her wet bathing suit. Their talk died to whispers, though, as she pulled out her flip-flops and backpack, then closed her locker door. With an inward sigh, she hoped the whispering and giggles did not mean their teenage venom was about to be directed at her.

"Hey, Dorsey, how's it going?" a voice asked over snickering in the background.

Dorsey turned to see the Wild Child standing there buck naked, dripping wet, hand on hip, her perfect seventeen-year-old body looking taut and perky except for a nasty scratch on her arm. She was halfway down the row of lockers, still a safe six feet from Dorsey, who coolly met her gaze and held it for a very long five seconds. Then, ignoring her completely, Dorsey glanced over at the other two, now silent.

"Hey, Kelly," she said pleasantly, "how's your dad?"

The hardware store and the Larue family were longtime customers of Mr. Blankenship's bank. The whole town knew he was currently in the hospital in Grover having gall bladder surgery.

"Oh, uh, fine," the girl said, coloring slightly and blinking in confusion at this unexpected turn of events.

Dorsey stuck her feet in her flip-flops, taking her time, then spoke to the third teenager, who'd been in the store with her mother not long ago buying a fancy coffeemaker. Jimalene gruffly affirmed the purchase was still satisfactory while failing to make eye contact and fidgeting with the handle on the door of her locker. Mariah was having a hard time holding her pose but didn't know what else to do. Dorsey picked up her backpack and walked out slowly, back ramrod straight. As the locker room door closed behind her, a gale of recriminations and bitchiness erupted from within as the Wild Child yelled at the other two for failing to support her. Score one for dignity and maturity, Dorsey thought, smiling to herself.

Great tits, though.

CHAPTER SEVEN

Ragged white clouds sailed through the midnight sky, alternately obscuring and revealing the moon. The promised rain had arrived late in the afternoon with violent thundershowers soaking the fields and the town. Dorsey emerged from her workshop to discover the rain had finally stopped. She'd made good progress on the dining room table she was building from scratch. An idea for the table had blossomed in her brain on the way home from the pool. She'd been so inspired she'd gone straight to the workshop without even bothering to shower off the chlorine. The table wasn't done yet, but she was already thinking ahead to the chairs that would accompany it. The dilapidated set of six matching chairs she'd picked up cheap at an estate sale would eventually form a cohesive unit with the table—each piece similar, but subtly different in such a way that a person's eye would be led from one to another only to come full circle and start the pattern again. This was one of her more ambitious projects, both in size and concept. She had no idea where the table and chairs would go once she finished the project, but that day's sale of the rocking chair to Dr. Melba was encouraging. Maybe her friend with the design store in Chicago would call.

And maybe not, she thought realistically. Still, she felt happy with the progress she'd made on the table that night. Seeing her artistic vision emerge from the wood was the most fulfilling thing she knew. She always felt refreshed and renewed after working in the shop, which technically belonged to all three of the Larue siblings. But she was the only one who really used the space and the tools. As much as she sometimes detested her life in Romeo Falls, she knew she could never leave the shop behind. Even if she could physically move the big heavy tools somewhere, where could she possibly keep them when she could barely afford an apartment for herself, let alone workshop space? It was a puzzle without an answer and a never-ending source of frustration.

She stretched, taking a deep breath of the rain-cleansed air and took a moment to admire the few stars that were visible amongst the clouds rushing above. Except for the breeze rustling the treetops and the dripping of rainwater from the leaves, all was quiet. The house was dark too, except for the kitchen light Goodman had left on for her. He was generally in bed by ten and back at the store no later than six. Shaw must have gone to bed too, she thought as she locked up the workshop and walked through the wet backyard toward the side door of the house, trying her best to avoid the bigger puddles.

A strange sound caught her attention. She paused, listening intently. There it was again. Coming from the front of the house. Not so much strange as out of place. It sounded like something small, but hard, hitting the roof, like the very first piece of pea-sized hail. She checked the sky again. Nope, not hailing in the backyard, so she seriously doubted it was in the front. Normally, she wouldn't have thought twice about it, but with all the weird things happening in town recently, she was feeling a little jumpy. Especially all by herself, outside, at midnight. Something pinged off one of the windows.

Dorsey crept silently toward the front of the house, keeping to the shadows. At the corner, she knelt down and carefully peeked around.

It was Sarah. Dorsey suddenly found it hard to breathe. What was Sarah doing on her front lawn at midnight, throwing pebbles at an unlit second-floor window? And managing to look absolutely gorgeous while doing so?

During first her lengthy swim and then in the workshop, Dorsey had had lots of time to think over their encounter from earlier in the day. Her head adamantly told her she had to break it off and the sooner, the better. But her heart told her otherwise. Damn it, she really liked Sarah. And she couldn't ignore the undeniable physical attraction between the two of them. "She'll break your heart," her head said. "Just one more kiss," countered her heart. Dorsey was torn, but in the end, pragmatic. Her friendship with Maggie was too important. What was probably, at best, a summer romance was not worth the risk of losing that lifelong friendship.

All of which sounded reasonable, but reason kept flying out the window every time she laid eyes on Sarah. Like now. Her soft, coal-black hair shimmered in the moonlight. The curves of her gorgeous body were accentuated by her close-fitting jeans and Henley shirt. Dorsey knew she'd be a goner once she'd looked into those amazing blue eyes again. How could she stop this thing between them when every cell in her body cried out for Sarah's touch?

"Dorsey!" Sarah hoarsely whispered into the night, aiming another pebble at the window. Dorsey didn't want to scare her, but she didn't see how she could avoid it. She stood up and stepped onto the lawn, ten feet from the other girl.

"Sarah," she said as quietly.

With a muffled exclamation, Sarah jumped, throwing her remaining fistful of pebbles wildly in the air. She whirled around.

"Sorry, sorry, it's me, it's Dorsey," she said softly, stepping further forward so Sarah could better see her in the dim light from the street.

"Holy crap, you scared me," Sarah told her, grabbing Dorsey's forearms tightly.

"What are you doing here?" Dorsey spoke barely above a whisper, to keep from waking her brothers and the neighbors.

"Trying to get your attention, obviously," Sarah whispered back.

"By throwing rocks at my little brother's window?"

"That's your *brother's* window? Shit. I thought it was yours."

Dorsey had, in fact, inhabited that second-floor bedroom as a child. In high school, she'd adorned the window with a rainbow sticker and some stained glass decals, which Shaw had never bothered to remove. Dorsey explained this to Sarah as they went in the front door.

"Your brother likes rainbow stickers?" Sarah asked in a whisper, following Dorsey through the dark living room to the kitchen.

"I don't think it's ever occurred to him to take them down. Shaw's kind of different," she said. Realizing that might have sounded bad, she hastily added, "He's really smart, though. Way smarter than I am, at least. He knows all about history and geography and stuff like that. I keep telling him he should go on *Jeopardy*, but he just laughs at me."

"Why?" Sarah said.

"Probably because he's never even been out of the state or on an airplane. And...well, he's just different. He's more of a dreamer than a doer, I guess. Or, I should say, he just has his own way of doing things."

Dorsey paused at the refrigerator, started to pull out two bottles of beer, then stopped and grabbed a bottle of wine and a corkscrew instead.

"Come on," Dorsey said, opening a door to the left of the fridge. "And grab two of those wineglasses, will you?"

"Where are you taking me?"

Dorsey flipped a switch, illuminating a carpeted stairwell.

"The basement," she said. "That's where my room is. We can talk down there."

As they went downstairs, Dorsey explained to Sarah how when their mother remarried and moved out, Goodman had taken over the master suite, she had moved down to the finished basement to have some privacy and Shaw took over her old room. She didn't add that all three of them now had their own bathrooms which greatly helped with domestic harmony. Also helping was the cleaning woman Good had hired to dust, mop and vacuum on a weekly basis. She probably made more cleaning houses than he did with the store, but it was well worth it to him. Good hated housework. Shaw's part was to take care of the yard and Dorsey was responsible for any repairs and general maintenance. It all worked out pretty smoothly.

The basement was quite large as it mirrored the footprint of the house. Sarah glanced curiously about her. The bare white walls and blue-gray indoor/outdoor carpeting weren't too impressive. Neither was the first view of the basement, which was strictly utilitarian. The visible half of it was one large open area, with the furnace, washer and dryer dominating the space. Several of Dorsey's completed projects were stored down there as well—a bookcase with glass-fronted doors, a Stickley-style recliner, a china hutch, various tables (sofa, end and coffee, among others), a door and at least a dozen large picture frames. Except for the projects she'd built from scratch, all the pieces had first been restored to their original splendor, then "re-imagined" in some way. Some pieces now had exotic wood inlaid with the original. For some, she'd taken a crucial design element and completely revamped it, like the legs on two of the tables. Whatever changes she'd made, her one rule was that the revitalized piece had to somehow artistically flow from the original. The results were arresting—sometimes quirky, sometimes downright odd, but beautiful and unique in their own way. At least Dorsey thought so.

"Wow," said Sarah, stopping in her tracks. "It's like an art gallery down here. This is amazing, Dorsey." She walked up to the china hutch and ran her fingertips over the hand-polished wood. "I can't believe people aren't lining up to buy this stuff from you."

Dorsey laughed, embarrassed but pleased. "Yeah, well, I'm so popular I'm starting to run out of room down here as you can see. Guess I need to make some more friends so I can at least give it away. You should take a piece with you when you leave town."

"Leave town? I'm not going anywhere," Sarah declared.

"Yeah, right," Dorsey said with a smile. "Like you're here to stay in good old Romeo 'Fails'? I don't think so, Sarah."

"Well, either way, I'd love to have one of your pieces someday when I have a place of my own again. I'm going to hold you to that."

"Whatever you want," Dorsey said, gesturing at the room. "Plus there's a dining room table and six chairs in the woodshop that I'm working on now. But it'll be a while before they're done."

"Tell you what, for right now, I'll settle for a glass of wine," Sarah told her. "But this can't be your room, can it?"

"Come on, I'll show you." Dorsey led her to a door in the wall that bisected the basement.

The other side was a whole different world. Hollis Larue had insulated and "finished" the basement in his lifetime, but Dorsey had done a lot of the work over the years on what was now her suite. It was originally intended to be a guest bedroom, complete with its own bath and a small living room as well. She had started by laying hardwood floors throughout. She'd acquired the wood for free when a century-old farmhouse deep in the countryside had been demolished. The furniture, of course, was all of her own devising. The plumbing and wiring she'd wisely left to the experts, although she'd learned a lot from hanging around and observing them at their crafts.

She was glad the cleaning lady had been there earlier in the day. The living room was gleaming and she knew the bathroom would be spotless too. She was neat and orderly by nature, but it was nice to know it was "company clean" for Sarah's unexpected visit.

"Very nice," her visitor said approvingly as she stepped over the threshold.

"Have a seat," Dorsey said, closing the door behind her. She joined Sarah on the sofa, but made sure there was at least a foot of space between them. She was still wrestling with her resolve to end things with Sarah. She just didn't know if she had the strength to do it now, with Sarah right there, sitting in her room. She'd imagined her—well, imagined the Naked Silver

Lake Goddess—there so many times, the reality threatened to overwhelm her.

"Won't Maggie be worried about you?" she asked Sarah as she poured them each a glass of white zinfandel.

"No, I left her a note that I was going out. Besides, she knows I sometimes go for a walk late at night if I can't sleep. And she can always call me on my cell phone if she needs me."

"So you walked over here?"

"Yeah," Sarah replied. "I figured a bright red Beetle in front of your house would get the neighbors talking."

"Uh, yeah, you got that right."

They both paused to take a sip of wine. Dorsey thought of the things she wanted to say. The things she needed to say. But she'd never been very good with words... She'd always been better with her hands. Sarah's eyes met Dorsey's.

Sarah said, "What were you going to do tonight if I hadn't shown up?"

"I don't know, probably just take a shower and go to bed, I guess," Dorsey answered truthfully and off the top of her head.

"Hmmm...so how can I help you with that?" Sarah asked with that devilish grin Dorsey was beginning to know so well.

Sarah's brilliant blue eyes gleamed at her. Dorsey felt a flare of desire deep within. She stood, not knowing what she was doing. Just one night, her heart said. Just give me this one night... give *us* this one night together... Sarah rose gracefully from the sofa as well. As if in a dream, Dorsey moved forward to take her in her arms. Still, something made her hesitate as she trembled on the brink.

"Are we making a mistake?" she said.

Sarah gazed seriously back at her.

"I think we both deserve a little happiness," she said softly. "Don't you?"

"So is this just for tonight?" Dorsey asked her. She wasn't sure what she wanted to hear. Did she herself want more than just one night? *You know you do,* her heart told her. *You belong together.* She'd never felt that way before about anyone. It scared her a little, but it felt so good.

Sarah said, "All I know is I want to be with you, Dorsey.

In your shower, in your bed, wherever you want. That's all I've wanted since that night at the festival—just to be with you again."

Their lips met as Dorsey pulled her in tight.

"That's all I want too," she murmured as she gently laid Sarah back down on the couch.

Candles flickered in the darkness as the soothing, sensual warmth of the shower cascaded down upon them. After making love on the sofa and then the living room floor, they'd finally made it to the shower in the wee hours of the morning.

Dorsey loved the way Sarah was taking her time on not just the obvious stuff, but everything—the backs of her knees, the tips of her fingers, the small of her back. She couldn't remember the last time she'd felt so stimulated by a woman's touch. Sarah's wet hands slid up her waist to gently caress Dorsey's breasts, her slick palms finding Dorsey's rock-hard nipples, teasing them with slow circles.

"So skinny," Sarah gently mocked her, eyes gleaming in the candlelight. "Your hips are like a boy's."

"Oh, yeah?" With a grin, Dorsey pinned her up against the wall of the shower. Sarah gasped at the coolness of the tile on her back. The gleam in her eyes deepened, her lips parting in surprise.

"I'm not a boy," Dorsey told her.

"Really?"

"Yeah."

"You better show me."

So she did.

Outside of Romeo Falls was open country, mostly fields with burgeoning crops of wheat, corn and alfalfa at that time of year. There were no streetlights out there. A car cruised slowly along the highway, its headlights the only illumination now that the moon had retreated behind a woolly blanket of clouds. There was no other traffic, not in the predawn hours of a weekday morning. The car, a nondescript family sedan, slowed to a stop in the middle of the road, its headlights converging on a sad little mound of fur. A dead possum. It was a big one, well over ten pounds by the look of it. The driver got out of the car, retrieving a shovel and a large plastic trash bag from the back of the vehicle. The possum was approached tentatively and poked first gingerly and then sharply with the shovel to make sure it really was dead. It was. The claws and the teeth were no longer any threat. There was little blood, but the neck was clearly broken, the pathetic little body clearly lifeless.

"I guess you'll have to do," the driver muttered, bending down with the trash bag.

CHAPTER EIGHT

Dorsey woke up at six like she always did, with or without the alarm clock. Although she'd only gotten a few hours of sleep, she felt marvelous. Refreshed, relaxed and energized, all at the same time. Her basement bedroom had a window near the top of one wall. A few stray beams of early morning sunshine were leaking through a gap in the curtains to spill across the sheet and patchwork quilt that covered her.

She'd forgotten what a pleasure it was to wake up the morning after having been so thoroughly touched, rubbed, stroked, caressed, licked, kissed and sucked to kingdom come the night before. So to speak.

So thoroughly *fucked*, she thought, stretching luxuriantly. She couldn't recall when she'd last felt so happy. She hazily remembered Sarah leaving sometime in the night. No doubt she wanted to be properly back at Chez Bigelow before sunrise. Dorsey noticed a folded slip of paper on the nightstand. She sat up and reached for it with a smile.

Dear Dorsey, she read, *I'm watching you sleep as I write this and you're so beautiful. I don't want to leave, but I have to. Until I see you again, all I'll be able to think of will be your skin on my skin, your lips on my lips...*

The note ended there. Breathlessly, she read it again. She even held it to her face to see if any lingering scent of Sarah remained behind. It didn't. She laughed at herself for acting like such a fool and jumped out of bed to get dressed and face the day. As she put on her jeans, the thought came to her that Sarah hadn't signed her note. That pulled her up short for a second. She read the note a third time. Then sighed. Was she already picking apart her moment of happiness, looking for signs and symbols that probably weren't there? She thrust the note into the back pocket of her jeans and resolved to be happy in the moment as best she could.

Goodman had already left and Shaw was not in evidence as she ate a bowl of cereal at the kitchen table. She wondered if he was still asleep upstairs. He was due at the store at seven thirty per the schedule on the refrigerator, so he'd better get a move on, she thought, wherever he was.

As if in response, the outside door to the kitchen opened and Shaw strolled in, looking mighty pleased with himself. He was wearing the same clothes he'd had on the day before and hadn't shaved. Clearly, he'd been out all night.

"Well, where have you been, buddy boy?" She felt a sisterly obligation to bust his chops at least a little bit.

Shaw shrugged and gave her a smile, but no reply. She grinned back. He went to the sink to wash his hands, then selected a bowl out of the drainer on the counter.

"So what's her name?" she persisted, more than a little curious. Hopefully not that youngest Lucchese girl, she thought. Shudder.

Shaw set down his bowl and picked up the two wineglasses that were in the sink. Dorsey had brought them up from the basement, intending to wash them with her breakfast dishes. He looked at the glasses speculatively, holding them up to the light and twirling them slowly. After shooting her a look, he set the glasses back down and joined her at the table, pouring cereal into his bowl.

"I guess I might ask you the same question," he said cheerfully.

The rest of breakfast time passed in a mutual and peaceful silence.

"So what do you think, Chief?"

Luke Bergstrom stared grimly at the hood of his police cruiser, which was parked in the driveway in front of his house. Officer Gargoyle's question didn't register. He was still engrossed in the fact that someone had defaced his vehicle in front of his house. While he was asleep in there, with his wife and his children. Luke prided himself on his professionalism and he wasn't showing anything but a bleak detachment to his subordinate, but he was deeply angry. Enraged, in fact.

"Chief?" Officer Gargoyle asked him again.

Both of them stared at the road kill gruesomely displayed on the hood of the car. It had been a possum, but was now more a collection of gory body parts. The severed head, the gutted torso, the tail and the extremities had been placed in the four quadrants defined by a large red X which was raggedly spray-painted on the hood. Flies buzzed around the sickening mess.

"Get the camera," Luke told her, rolling up his sleeves methodically. "Get it all—pictures, prints, bag the evidence, you know the drill."

"You got it," she said. She was as incensed as he was by this insult to their department, but she was excited as well. This was different than the usual moving violations, drunken fights and petty thefts she normally dealt with.

"It's getting worse, isn't it, Luke?" she asked him.

"Yeah," he said. "Like somebody is working up to something."

"Like what?" Gargoyle said.

He stared at her for a moment, his eyes narrowed, his face like stone.

"I wish I knew," he said.

The next seven days were the happiest week of Dorsey's life. She and Sarah found many opportunities to spend time together, both with and without Maggie, who'd been reluctantly pulled into teaching a few days of summer school classes for a sick colleague. On one of those days, Sarah joined Dorsey out at the Bartholomews' place, where the deck was nearing completion. The freedom of knowing they were alone and no one else was around for miles was exhilarating. They made love in the hayloft above the barn as an afternoon rain shower softly fell.

"Is that big goofy grin all for me?" Sarah teased her as they lay in each other's arms afterward, contentedly spooning on a blanket and listening to the raindrops on the roof. She was propped up on one elbow, gazing down at Dorsey's face.

Dorsey turned to her. "It's for you," she agreed. "And for me too. I just feel so happy when I'm with you."

Sarah charmingly blushed and pulled Dorsey in close. "You make me happy too," she said, making Dorsey's heart skip a beat.

"Tell me something about yourself that I don't know," Sarah said impulsively.

"Like what?"

"Like...I don't know...tell me about your first time."

"Oh my God," Dorsey said, laying back and putting both hands behind her head. "Do we really have to go there?" But she was laughing.

"Come on," Sarah said persuasively. "You tell me yours and I'll tell you mine."

"Well...all right," Dorsey said. "When I was in high school, I used to go to this swim camp in the summer. The summer I was seventeen, I was a junior camp counselor. And there was this older girl—"

"Let me guess," Sarah interrupted. "She wasn't the *head* counselor, by any chance, now was she?"

"Hey, whose story is this?" Dorsey objected, laughing. "Well, long story short, she was a college girl, one of the senior counselors and...well, let's just say she greatly improved my stroke technique."

"I'll bet," Sarah said dryly. "Did Maggie go to this camp with you?"

"No, Maggie's not much of a swimmer. Plus, she hates being seen in a bathing suit, in case you haven't noticed."

"Yeah, I've noticed."

The mention of Maggie seemed to cast a bit of a pall over their golden afternoon. Sarah tried to gloss over it with another breezy comment.

"Just think, Dorse, if I'd come here when I was a kid, then I could have been your older woman instead of that hussy at the swim camp."

She'd meant it as a joke, but Dorsey looked back at her seriously. "And if you had," she said, "then Maggie would know you're gay."

Sarah looked away, the smile on her lips fading.

"I just hate keeping this secret from her," Dorsey said, wanting Sarah to understand. Wanting her to come out to Maggie, so there'd be no more lying, no more deception. If they could just work it out with her, how perfect would that be, Dorsey thought. She and Maggie could be almost like sisters-in-law, she thought dreamily...

But Sarah sat up and started to get dressed. "I know," she said to Dorsey. "And I want to tell her—but when the moment is right, you know? I just...can't we just take a little time for ourselves to be happy? Is that so selfish?" She looked pleadingly at Dorsey. "Just give me some time, Dorsey. Give *us* some time."

"Okay," Dorsey said, relenting. What else could she do?

CHAPTER NINE

Luke sat at his desk in the police station, reviewing some of the never-ending paperwork that was almost a bigger part of his job than the actual crime-stopping. Fortunately, it had been a slow week for crime, even by Romeo Falls' standards: a couple of domestic spats, a non-injury car wreck and some teenagers trying to inveigle their elders into buying them beer at the liquor store.

No vandalism. Luke grunted to himself and shifted in his chair. He wished he felt easier in his mind about that. His gut told him the string of malicious incidents wasn't over yet, despite the lack of activity on that front the past week. Frustratingly, they were no closer to capturing the miscreant, whoever he or she might be. From the lack of fingerprints or other giveaway clues, it almost seemed like the perpetrator was familiar with police procedure. Of course, that was true of just about anybody who turned on a TV these days. An eyewitness would be helpful, but the perp had been smart enough, or lucky enough, to avoid that so far too. The smear of blood on the church sign was the most promising potential link so far, but without someone to compare it to, it was useless for the moment.

It wasn't like any of the incidents was that big a crime, in and of itself. A little graffiti. Some beheaded flowers. A vandalized church sign. The gutted possum on the squad car was the nastiest, no doubt about it. Still, they all added up to not much more than petty high school level bullshit, really. He had his eye on various local punks and punkettes, but the creep had managed to stay just out of his reach. Even if it was just a string of dirty tricks, Luke hated the idea of somebody getting away with it in his town. He could feel whoever it was laughing at him and it pissed him off.

And was it someone local? At this point, he didn't know. Maggie's cousin Sarah was still a question mark in his mind. But that was because of what he *didn't* know about her, not what he did. Based on what he'd personally observed, she was an intelligent, attractive young woman who was in town to visit her relatives, just like she had told him. The information he'd gotten from his buddy in Chicago he categorized more as a rumor than solid fact. A rumor of an unstable love affair that ended badly, a mere hint of a suggestion about drug use... As a cop, he was used to sorting rumor from fact. The jury was still out on Sarah, he'd decided.

The only other stranger in town, so to speak, was the new doctor, Melba Porter, although she'd been there six months already. After their old doctor finally retired, the town had been grateful to find a new, not to mention young, physician willing to move to Romeo Falls and treat their various ills. Of course, there were questions, as always, when a newcomer arrived. Why had she chosen their tiny town? She wasn't even from the same state. Why not stay in Chicago where she'd gone to school and go for the big bucks?

As he mulled the possibilities, Officer Gargoyle appeared in his office doorway. "Fax for you, Chief," she said, handing him some sheets of paper. "From Chicago PD."

"Thanks," he told her. He viewed the fax with interest. It was a response to an inquiry he'd initiated a few days earlier. The confidential document was copies of pages from a closed case file which was several years old. The subject of the fax was not the person whose name appeared on that case file, but a peripheral player in the story it described.

"...*a twenty-seven-year-old white female intern at Queen of the Plains Medical Center in Chicago...*"

Luke skimmed the fax, looking for the information he specifically sought.

"...*after further investigation, it appears the intern, Melba Desiree* (Desiree? thought Luke) *Porter was under severe financial and emotional stress at the time she was approached by the subject in an attempt to illegally procure prescription narcotics with her assistance. Subject is a friend of her brother who is well known to this investigator. Porter met with the subject on two occasions, but refused his requests, eventually breaking off all contact with him after their second meeting...*"

"Way to go, Dr. Melba," Luke murmured under his breath. He flipped to the next page of the fax.

"...*during that interrogation, subject admitted he had attempted to blackmail Dr. Porter by threatening to make public her brother's involvement in various illegal activities...*"

Luke turned to the final page, which was dated some months later than the other ones.

"...*the possible extortion charge was dropped, however, when Dr. Porter was unavailable to testify against the subject...on extended and indefinite leave of absence from Queen of the Plains...inpatient treatment at a private psychiatric facility for what was described as 'mental and physical exhaustion'...*"

And that was it. There was no further mention of Dr. Melba (or of any other Romeo Falls resident) in the fax. She obviously had returned to her job and completed her residency, or she wouldn't be practicing in Romeo Falls now. Luke made a mental note to double-check on that. If nothing else, the fax shed some light, perhaps, on why she had left Chicago for a much smaller and slower paced community. But did it have any relevance to the events taking place now in his town? Probably not, he thought, as he filed the fax away in a locked cabinet in his office.

Patience, he told himself, patience. Sometimes his job reminded him of a football game. Waiting for the offense to hike the ball, so he and the rest of the defense could react. He didn't know who was calling the plays this time, so all he could do was wait. And hope he'd be ready for his opponent's next move.

On Thursday afternoon, Dorsey was at work when the phone rang.

"Larue's Swingtime Hardware, Dorsey speaking," she answered cheerfully. Even if she hadn't been feeling cheerful already, she would have answered that way since Good was standing right there. Outstanding customer service, one hundred percent of the time, whether on the phone or in person, was high on Goodman's list of priorities.

"I've got two hours," Sarah's voice said conspiratorially in her ear.

Dorsey looked at her watch: fifteen minutes before five. Almost closing time. She glanced at her brother, who was behind the counter with her, sitting on the stool and filling out some paperwork for a vendor.

"Yes, ma'am, we close at five," she said with a smile into the phone, "but I can arrange for a delivery to your home if that's more convenient."

"Not here," Sarah replied.

Dorsey could hear the grin in her voice, could feel the kick she was getting out of their little game. Much like the excitement Dorsey felt building inside herself. "Tell you what—I'll meet you behind the store in half an hour. Does that work for you?"

Goodman glanced at her incuriously, probably wondering who was on the phone, then went back to his paperwork.

"Yes, ma'am," Dorsey said again. "I'll be happy to help you out with that. And thank you for calling Larues!"

There was a slight pause on the other end. Dorsey could picture Sarah on the wall-mounted phone in the Bigelow kitchen, hands cupped around the receiver, eyes aglow and darting around to make sure she was alone for the moment.

"I can't wait to taste you," she said in her huskiest whisper.

"Yes, I believe I have what you need," Dorsey replied with a poker face. "Whether it's inside or out."

She wasn't sure if that last line actually made any sense, but it had sounded good in her head. And had made Sarah laugh, which always filled her with a warm glow.

"See you in thirty," Sarah said and hung up.

It didn't take much convincing to get Good to let her close up the store. He grunted a surprised thanks, then took his paperwork with him, saying he wanted nothing more than to go home, relax and watch the ball game. She knew he would work on the paperwork while he watched. After he left, she finished closing up and set the alarm, then went out the back door into the alley where she'd parked that morning.

Sarah was sitting on the hood of Dorsey's little pickup truck, smiling at her in a way that made her feel almost dizzy with happiness. Happy that someone else was actually happy to see her. Happy to see the woman who had taken over her dreams and most of her waking thoughts as well.

The object of her adoration was looking pretty damn adorable, as a matter of fact. Her outfit was simple—jeans, sneakers and a tight-fitting, hot pink T-shirt—but showed off her body in a way that had Dorsey's heart hammering. She took Sarah's outstretched hand and pulled her off the truck and into her arms in one quick fluid motion. She wanted nothing more than to kiss her, but it wasn't safe even in the shelter of the alley. Someone might walk by at any moment. Even a hug in broad daylight was risky, she knew, but she couldn't resist. As she reveled in the sweet sensation of Sarah's body against hers, she held onto her for an extra moment or two, savoring the intensity of her feelings, waiting for the overpowering hunger in her to almost—almost—crest.

"I want to be alone with you," Sarah whispered in her ear.

Dorsey took a deep breath and released her.

"Me, too," she said. "But—can we maybe walk around the square or something? I've been cooped up in the store all day and I feel like I need a breath of fresh air before I go back indoors."

"Okay, Nature Girl," Sarah said laughingly. She entwined her arm in Dorsey's and they walked down the alley to the street. As they rounded the corner, Dorsey slipped her arm out of Sarah's and made sure they were walking at least six inches apart.

"Hey," Sarah complained and reached for her hand.

"We can't," Dorsey reminded her in an undertone. "Not here, not in the daylight."

"Come on, who's going to see us?"

She was right, in that there were very few people either walking or driving around the square at that moment. The stores and offices all closed at five. Just about everybody was home for dinner already or on their way. Dorsey wondered again at Sarah's sometimes conflicting behavior. She still hadn't found a way to come out to Maggie—but here she was, practically ready to make out on Main Street. Dorsey shook her head in confusion as they passed the movie theater, which was dark and shuttered on a weekday evening. Matinees were Saturdays only. They'd open up later for the seven o'clock weeknight show.

Sarah drew her into the shadows of the entryway, ostensibly to look at the posters for the upcoming flicks. She paused by one advertising a steamy jungle epic with a bare-chested hero and scantily clad girl clinging together as a tiger, a variety of snakes and some annoyed-looking natives menaced them.

"Wow, and I thought I had problems," Sarah laughed as they looked at it. Dorsey turned to smile at her and that was it— their eyes met and Sarah leaned in close, her hand on Dorsey's forearm, her lips just brushing Dorsey's...

The half-full beer can smacked against the wall above their heads, then ricocheted into a corner. The squealing of truck tires, braying, drunken laughter and a shouted "Burn in hell, you bulldykes!" echoed about them in the entryway. They heard the truck speed away without ever getting a look at their attackers. Dorsey ran her hands down her shirt in disgust to wipe off a few drops of beer.

"Are you all right?" she said to Sarah, who was pale and shaking, more from fury than fright.

"Son of a bitch," she snarled. "Did you see who threw it?"

"No," Dorsey said. "It doesn't matter. Look, we better get moving before they come back again."

"What do you mean, it doesn't matter?" Sarah demanded heatedly as they eased their way past the box office and back into the open. Dorsey made sure the coast was clear before they proceeded. Sarah was still venting her rage. "That was an assault, Dorsey. If you know who it was, then I'm calling the cops."

"No need," Dorsey said with a sinking heart. "She's already here."

Officer Gargoyle braked her patrol car to an abrupt stop at the curb in front of them, with a chirp of the tires and an entirely unnecessary *whoop* from the siren as well. She turned on the blue lights—again unnecessarily, Dorsey thought, as she was parked in a space, not blocking traffic. Gargoyle ponderously removed herself from her vehicle, adjusting her gun belt as she swaggered toward them.

"What's going on here?" she said loudly and officiously.

A merchant sweeping the sidewalk in front of his store on the opposite side of the square stopped to watch. A car waiting at the stoplight didn't move although the light was green, its driver and passengers gawking at them. Gargoyle spotted the beer can in the corner beneath the movie poster.

"It's illegal to have an open container in public," she told them, whipping out her little citation notebook.

Sarah said angrily, "Are you crazy? That's not ours. Some goddamn redneck just threw that at us. They're the ones you need to be talking to."

Gargoyle paused in the act of flipping open her notebook and stared at Sarah, her mean little eyes narrowed as she considered her next move.

"Now why would someone do that?" she asked. "Just what were you two doing in there anyhow?"

"Looking at the movie posters," Sarah replied, outraged. "What do you think we were doing?"

Dorsey touched Sarah's wrist, trying to get her attention and make her stop talking. There was no way Gargoyle was going to help them, she knew. She felt embarrassed—not for herself or Sarah, but for her town. If Sarah kept talking, she might find herself on the wrong end of a ticket or worse.

Sarah stared at her furiously when she felt her touch on her wrist. "What?" she demanded.

And Gargoyle was looking at her, too, with a look that Dorsey knew all too well. A look of revulsion, of hatred, of fear and ignorance...no doubt the same look as on the faces of the people in the pickup truck who'd thrown the beer at them.

Speaking of which, the sound of a big engine accelerating came to Dorsey's ears. She turned toward the direction it was coming from, but the early evening sun was shining right in her eyes. She saw a late-model full-size pickup, maybe black or dark blue, careen around the corner back into the square, music blaring out its open windows, a flannel-sleeved arm protruding from the passenger side window, beer can at the ready. Dorsey grabbed Sarah and ducked back into the marginal shelter of the theater entryway, but the thrower's aim was off. The beer can—an almost full one by the sound of it—bounced off the back of Officer Gargoyle's patrol car and rolled harmlessly into the gutter, where it lay sputtering and foaming.

"Fuckin' lezzie perverts!" was the curse screamed at them this time. The pickup truck sped off.

"Oh HELL no," Gargoyle said, more to herself than to them and obviously referring to the insult to her car, not the enmity aimed at them. She hitched up her belt and headed for her car at speed, pausing only to point two fingers back at Sarah and Dorsey. "I've got my eyes on you, missy," she said to Sarah, then crammed herself back under the wheel, and set off with the siren shrieking and lights a-flashing.

"Are you kidding me?" Sarah said in disbelief to Dorsey, who almost wanted to laugh if it weren't all so unfunny.

"Come on," she told Sarah. "Let's get out of here before either one of them comes back."

They walked quickly back to the alley behind the hardware store. A light rain had started to fall, which further sped them on their way. By the time they got to Dorsey's truck, the ludicrousness of the situation had overtaken them. They were both laughing and out of breath as they piled into the little pickup. Dorsey put the key in the ignition, then said to Sarah, "So where are we going?"

Before she could answer, a sudden sharp clash of thunder made them both jump and check the sky, which had been at least partially blue just moments before.

"Whoa," Sarah said apprehensively. "That doesn't look good."

It had been raining on and off the entire day, but now the sky had taken on that eerie greenish tone seen only in the midwest. Thunder rumbled again in the distance, but they hadn't seen any lightning. The storm was still miles away, but storms could move frighteningly fast over the open prairie. They needed to find some safe place indoors and soon.

George and Ira obviously agreed about the indoors part. The cats had been out and about in town, but as the women watched, they ran down the alley with alacrity, tails straight up in the air, and zipped in through the kitty door.

"We need to get inside somewhere too," Dorsey told Sarah. "That sky's not looking good."

"Someplace where we can be alone," Sarah agreed with her. She reached out to lightly trace the back of Dorsey's hand on the stick shift. Even that small contact triggered the fierce and aching desire that Dorsey felt whenever Sarah was with her. That desire could not be delayed another hour. She wanted Sarah—needed Sarah—now, not later. And the look in Sarah's eyes told her she felt exactly the same way.

"Your place?" Sarah said.

"Well..." Dorsey hesitated. "Goodman's there, so not really. I don't suppose your place..."

"No, their women's group is assembling some ghastly craft project in what seems like every room of the house. That's what made me flee in the first place."

They both glanced up at the sky with a sense of urgency. Ominous pewter-gray clouds were stacking up into thunderheads as they watched. A flock of birds wheeled past, darting and diving through the sky in search of a tree or a building where they could ride out whatever was coming.

"Motel?" Sarah suggested, a little desperately.

"No good," Dorsey said. "It's owned by the Luccheses."

Seeing Sarah's look of noncomprehension, she added, "Those drunken heifers at The Hamlet, remember?"

"Oh. Well, what about the store?" she said pragmatically, pointing at the back door just ten feet away. More fat raindrops were starting to splatter down onto the pavement. It wouldn't be long before the skies opened up with a vengeance.

As a place to take shelter in from the elements, the store was an excellent option. As a place to get laid in, not so much. For one thing, she was fairly certain Good would kill her if he ever found out. Plus, the idea of it felt a little strange. She'd grown up in that store. She'd grown up in her house too, of course, but a house has bedrooms and bedrooms are for having sex in. Not hardware stores.

But she had no choice. The first piece of hail pinged off the hood of the truck as she sat there dithering.

"All right," she told Sarah. "Let's go!"

They ran for the door. Dorsey fumbled with the keys, then got them inside just as the first heavy wall of rain came racing down from the heavens.

They were in the back of the store, the windowless stockroom, with all manner of boxes and bags stacked around them. Dorsey flicked the light switch, but the power had already gone out—not unusual when it was storming. Fortunately, the keypad for the alarm system was lighted by a back-up battery, so she was able to quickly disarm it.

"Hold on," she told Sarah, who was clinging tightly to Dorsey's chambray shirt so she wouldn't lose her in the dark. Dorsey knew the layout of the store like the back of her hand and could have navigated it blindfolded, which was good considering that was essentially what she was having to do. It was close to pitch-black in there as the storm closed in. The rain was roaring outside, hail banging on the roof, with thunder now bone-jarringly close and ever more frequent. Dorsey was headed to the front counter, where there was a flashlight under the cash register.

"Wait," Sarah said to her as they passed the open doorway of the office, murkily sensed rather than seen in the near total darkness of the hall. "Office?"

The office was so completely Goodman's domain that the idea of getting it on in there was not appealing. At all. Besides, Dorsey had a better idea.

"Nope," she told Sarah. "Come on, we're almost there."

"I have to be back for dinner by seven," Sarah warned her.

"Almost there," Dorsey promised, pulling her forward.

In the back corner of the store, far from the plate glass window which stretched all the way across the front, Goodman had dedicated a small area to patio furniture and other outdoor items. Dorsey carefully guided Sarah to a chair and sat her down.

"I'll be right back," she told her. Sarah's fingers reluctantly released her.

"Hurry," she whispered fiercely.

Dorsey moved as quickly as she could through the dark and silent store, its internal quietness in stark contrast to the racket Mother Nature was making outside. She found the flashlight under the cash register, where both the cats were huddled together, green eyes aglow in the near total darkness. She petted Ira, got a hiss from George for daring to make eye contact, then detoured to the front window where an old family quilt was draped over one of her furniture pieces as part of the display. Rain lashed the front window violently and she could see the water running high in the street outside in what was left of the daylight.

She hurried back to Sarah, who impatiently stood when she saw the small beam of the flashlight headed toward her.

"Okay, so we got a chair, a flashlight and a quilt," she said to Dorsey, adding up their assets like a castaway on a desert island. "What else? Plenty of tools and hardware. Tools...hmmm, so how do you feel about tools, Dorsey?"

Sarah's tone of voice had changed from pragmatic to sultry. Her warm hands were now wandering over Dorsey's torso as she put the flashlight and quilt down on the patio table next to the chair. Sarah was nibbling on her neck, pressed up against her from behind, not letting her straighten back up from her bent over position at the table. Which felt rather nice, actually. Sarah's hand slipped down the outside front of Dorsey's jeans until her firm grip found a home. A sharp wave of desire filled Dorsey with heat, suffusing her from head to toe as her body moved with Sarah's dominating hand. She found herself gasping for breath, gripping the table with all her might.

"Tools?"

"Tools, toys, accoutrements," Sarah breathed in Dorsey's ear. "You know. I bet we could get real creative with some of the stuff in this store if we wanted to."

Dorsey had been more than gratified with the creativity already shown by Sarah in their short time together. There was much more to explore, she knew, and she was definitely looking forward to that in time, but for now—even with her wholesale discount—she thought it wiser to stick with the tried-and-true.

"Ummm, yeah," she managed, finally squirming out of Sarah's embrace. "I've got something else in mind for this afternoon," she told Sarah, who was taking advantage of their temporary uncoupling to start peeling off her clothes. Dorsey picked up the quilt and flashlight and turned on a battery operated camping lantern on the table. Its gentle light bathed Sarah in a golden glow as she dexterously dropped her bra on the pile of her other clothes, then gracefully shimmied out of her panties as Dorsey watched, her anticipation mounting almost painfully. She'd never felt this way before, never wanted another woman this badly.

"Well," Sarah said, posing for her for a moment with her hand saucily on her hip. "What exactly did you have in mind?"

Dorsey had lost the power of speech when the bra came off, so she merely turned and mutely shone her flashlight into the corner behind the patio furniture, where a four-person tent stood, flap unzipped and inviting, with sleeping bags and a faux plastic, molded campfire to complete the picture.

She would never think of camping the same way, she thought, as she followed Sarah's pale and perfect buttocks into the cozy little tent.

CHAPTER TEN

Dorsey and Maggie had lunch together that Friday, which was Maggie's last day as a substitute teacher. Her colleague had recovered from whatever bug had afflicted him and was due back in the classroom on Monday. Since her last day was actually just a half-day, Maggie was celebrating with a well-earned glass of wine with her lunch at the Blue Duck. Dorsey enjoyed her cheeseburger and her break from work while Maggie brought her up to speed on all the latest.

"And Mother and I are off to the capital this weekend for the state convention," she finished as Dorsey started on her fries.

"How is your mother?" Dorsey asked dutifully.

"Well, her ankle's still bothering her some. She had Sarah run her over to the clinic in Grover today for a follow-up appointment."

Dorsey actually knew that already, having had to cancel a planned rendezvous with Sarah as a result of Mrs. Bigelow's commandeering of the red Bug and its driver. She felt an uneasy twinge of guilt when Maggie told her what she already knew.

She knew all about the convention Maggie mentioned as well. Both the Bigelows belonged to a women's organization that was a social hub for the churchgoing ladies in town. Maggie was currently the treasurer, while her mother was the recording secretary. Tanya Hartwell was the president. Although Dorsey's mother had been a member, Dorsey herself had never been asked to join, for which she was deeply grateful. Mrs. Bigelow and Mags had been thrilled when they were chosen to be the representatives from Romeo Falls at the annual state convention that year and had been looking forward to a swinging weekend at the capital Best Western.

Dorsey said, "So y'all are still going despite her ankle problem?"

"Yep, we're going," Maggie assured her. "We're leaving as soon as her soap opera is done this afternoon. Wild horses couldn't keep Mother away from convention. She's on the rules and regulations committee this year, you know."

Dorsey nodded politely while thinking how perfect that was for the old she-beast. She reached for her Coke and took a long sip. She hoped she didn't sound like she was *too* eager for Maggie to go. On the one hand, of course she wanted her to go and enjoy herself and have a good time. And on the other hand, she very much wanted her to be gone so she could be alone with Sarah. It was all very confusing. With each encounter she and Sarah had, the guilt was ratcheting up in Dorsey's conscience. She hated having this secret from Maggie. But it wasn't her secret so much as it was Sarah's and if Sarah wasn't ready to tell Maggie, neither could she. Such a mess...

"Dorse? You with me?" Maggie smiled at her forgivingly, amused at her distracted state.

"I'm sorry—what?"

"I said, so I guess you and Sarah will just have to cope without us for a couple of days."

Dorsey choked on her drink, for no reason whatsoever, except her guilt-stricken conscience.

"I'm all right, I'm all right," she said to Maggie's concerned face. She coughed into her napkin, then took another long pull on her drink.

"You'll keep an eye on her for me, won't you?" Maggie said. "I've been kind of worried about leaving her alone for the weekend. She was so unhappy when she first got here. She didn't tell me much about what happened in Chicago, but I know it must have been hard for her, breaking up with her boyfriend like that."

Coca-Cola again went down the wrong pipe. Dorsey grabbed for her napkin, her eyes wet as she coughed.

"Sorry," she said weakly to Maggie, coughing and waving her hand in a go-ahead gesture. "You were saying? About a... boyfriend? Is that what Sarah told you?"

"Well, not in so many words," Maggie replied, "but I think I know a broken heart when I see one."

Dorsey pondered that in silence.

"She's never really talked about her love life much," Maggie said. "She's pretty private that way. Kind of like you in that regard," she added with a twist to her lips.

Wake up, Mags! Dorsey wanted to shout.

"Anyway," Maggie went on, "I just wanted to tell you how happy I am that you two have become friends now. It means so much to me."

Dorsey squirmed in her seat, wretchedly wishing she could tell Maggie the truth right here, right now and get it over with. Maggie seemed oblivious to her distress. She leaned over the table to tell Dorsey something confidentially.

"I'm only telling you this because I know you would never pass it on and because I know you care about Sarah too—you know those pills she got from the pharmacy? Well, they're antidepressants."

Dorsey was a bit taken aback by that news, but felt like she should defend Sarah. Which was odd, considering it was Maggie she was talking to.

"Well, you know a lot of people take those pills these days,

Mags," she said evenly. "It doesn't have to be a big deal. She said they helped her sleep, right?"

"I know," Maggie said, "but I've just been worried about her. She gets these dark moods sometimes and goes all quiet on me. That's why I'm glad you'll be here with her this weekend so she won't get lonely."

"Yeah, okay," Dorsey said, hoping to move on to other topics.

"You two have plans, right?" Maggie persisted.

Since Dorsey's plan was to get Sarah naked and fuck her brains out all weekend long, she couldn't exactly share that with Maggie. Nor could she share their escapades in a hotel room in Grover earlier in the week...or in the cab of her truck that one night out on a deserted country road after she had shown Sarah the falls for which the town was named...

"Dorse?" Maggie looked at her oddly when she again didn't answer right away.

"We'll be fine, Mags. I'll take good care of her, I promise."

"That's all I needed to hear," said Maggie, beaming. She flagged down the passing waitress and asked for the dessert menu.

The Miscreant was filling up at the gas station. And thinking. There were so many possibilities to think about as the next move was planned. And the planning was almost as much fun as the doing. So many possible targets. The high school, maybe. A perfect example of what was wrong with this stupid little town. That would show those losers... Or the community center. Maybe something completely off the wall, like the Blue Duck. Not that there was anything wrong with the place, but the very randomness of the choice was appealing.

The ticking of the gas pump seemed in time with the thoughts tumbling one over another. Maybe a person, instead of a place? Maybe just randomly pick one of these people...these fucking smug, self-satisfied, stuck-up assholes who thought they were so much better...anything to wake them up from their cozy little comatose lives.

The heady smell of the fuel sparked another thought. How about a fire? That would wake them up, for sure. That would leave a mark on this sorry-ass town they wouldn't soon forget! Go out in a blaze of glory, like they say...I'd torch this whole goddamn town if I could, thought the Miscreant.

Dorsey had worked all day in the store on Friday, but she was uncharacteristically absentminded the closer the clock got to closing time. Her brain kept thinking about the night ahead. A night in which she'd have Sarah all to herself. All night long...

"Dorsey!" Goodman barked at her exasperatedly from behind the counter as she stared dreamily out the front window. "Would you please set up that duct tape display in aisle two? I've asked you about four times already."

"Sorry, Good," she said contritely. "I'll do it right now."

She forced herself to concentrate on putting together the cardboard display rack provided by the manufacturer. Tab B absolutely refused to go into Slot C, but she finally overcame the design flaw with—what else?—a little duct tape. Having neatly stacked the display with different colored rolls of tape, she grabbed the push broom and swept for a while as her brothers dealt with the customers. The clock moved slowly. She felt like she'd been there for at least the duration of a geological epoch when closing time finally came around. She had hoped Good would let her go first, but saw to her dismay that Shaw had already beaten her to it.

"Where's he going?" she asked with chagrin as their younger brother disappeared out the front door.

"He said he's got a date and plus he's opening tomorrow, so I let him go early," Goodman answered. "You don't mind closing, do you? I promised old man Gustafson I'd run a delivery out to him this evening."

Crap, Dorsey thought. "Well, to tell you the truth, Good—"

"Thanks, Dorse! I'm going to Grover after—I told you that,

right?" Seeing her questioning look, he added, "It's Spider's birthday party, remember?" Spider was one of his old football buddies, who now lived in GC. "So I'll see you tomorrow, okay?"

"Okay," she said, but he was already headed out the back to his truck.

Well, with Goodman off in Grover City for one of his rare nights out and Shaw on a date with his mystery woman, it looked like she and Sarah would have the house to themselves. She felt the blood quicken in her veins as she contemplated the night ahead.

She sped through the various closing-up-the-store tasks, including feeding the kitties and making sure they had fresh water in their bowls for the night. Dorsey knew better than to pet George, but she gave Ira a friendly scratch under the chin by way of a goodnight to him. He meowed loudly once from his perch on the counter next to the cash register as she turned out all the lights but one, then locked the front door as she exited.

Sarah was due to meet her at the Larue house, where Dorsey was going to prepare dinner for the two of them. She steered her little pickup over to the grocery store on her way home to pick up a few last-minute ingredients. She'd spent hours—days, actually—deciding what to cook. She felt a little nervous about cooking for Sarah for the first time. She liked cooking, but she didn't do it often enough to have attained much skill at it. She didn't kid herself that she was on the level of either Maggie or Mrs. Bigelow, both of whom were excellent cooks. Sarah had assured her she wasn't picky and that anything she made would be fine, but Dorsey was still having her doubts. She'd finally fallen back on her own mother's favorite recipe for chicken Kiev.

Oh, well, she thought, as she picked up the next to last of her items. Even if she screwed it up, Sarah would still know she had tried. Maybe it was better for her to find out sooner rather than later that Dorsey wasn't quite a gourmet chef. Then she caught herself—thinking wow, was that a "long-term commitment" kind of thought? She wasn't sure. She'd never had one of those before. Musing on this, she rounded the corner to the wine and beer aisle, wanting to pick up an extra bottle of the white zinfandel

Sarah had identified as her favorite. To Dorsey's surprise, Shaw was there, standing perplexedly in front of the reds.

"Hey, bud, what are you doing here?" she asked him, even as her eyes widened to marvel at his outfit—a clean pair of khaki cargo pants, a white button-down dress shirt with the sleeves rolled up and (wonder o' wonders!) a tie. Which, on closer inspection, featured Snoopy as Joe Cool on a brilliant blue background (he must have picked that up at the thrift store in Grover, she thought), but was nonetheless undeniably A Tie. A pair of dark brown chukka boots completed the ensemble, which, for Shaw, was about as dressed up as he ever got.

"Which one of these should I get?" he asked her, gesturing at the array of bottles on the shelves with puzzlement.

"How the heck should I know?" she said. "Pick something that costs more than five bucks if you're trying to impress her, I guess. And who is 'her,' by the way?"

Shaw gave her a smile, but no reply. He selected a fifteen dollar bottle with a gorgeous label from a Napa Valley winery, then held it up for her inspection.

"Hot stuff," Dorsey kidded him.

She added a bottle of the white zinfandel to her cart, then the two of them walked to the checkout stand. They chatted amiably about nothing much as the cashier rang up their purchases.

"Do you need a ride somewhere?" she asked her brother as they headed for the exit.

"No," he replied. "I've got my bike."

Shaw had no vehicle of his own, although Goodman let him drive the store pickup on occasion. He turned left toward the bike rack as they went out the door, while Dorsey walked to her truck, which was parked in the second row. As she put her bags onto the passenger seat, she could see Shaw riding off with his wine bottle in its skinny brown bag tucked under one arm. Walking back to the driver's side, she heard a shout.

"Watch where you're going, La Puke!"

An angry Justin Argyle was picking himself up off the sidewalk in front of the store. Shaw too, was on the ground, in a tangle of long legs, bicycle and brown bag. A spreading puddle of red wine was underneath him. Dorsey ran to his side as Shaw regained his feet.

"Are you all right, Shaw?"

"Shit," he said with feeling. His shirt was spattered with red, his pants less so. The wine bottle was obviously broken. A spoke on his bicycle's front wheel was also broken, pointing accusingly at Justin, who was in Shaw's face and aggressively berating him.

"What the fuck do you think you're doing, La Puke? You fucking ran me over, you faggot!"

He pushed Shaw in the chest. Shaw's feet got tangled up in the fallen bicycle and he went down hard again on the pavement.

"That's enough, Justin!" Dorsey said, stepping up to face him and forestall any further violence. "It was an accident."

Justin glared at her, his eyes narrowed and red, his nostrils flared. Dorsey could smell beer and cigarettes on his breath. He was unshaven and unkempt in appearance. His customary denim jacket looked dirtier than ever. One of the sleeves was ripped, adding to his air of shabbiness. Dorsey stared him down, wondering if he was crazy enough to hit her right in public. He seemed to be considering that option, but before he could act on it, the store manager came running out the front in his bow tie and red apron.

"What's going on here?"

A few other shoppers had gathered as well. Dorsey took a step back from Justin, who still stood there glaring and breathing heavily. She unclenched her fist from around her car keys—the truck key stuck out between her index and third fingers. One thing she had learned growing up with two brothers—not to mention dealing with the Tanya Hartwells of the world—was that fighting dirty in defense of oneself was not only okay, it was often the quickest and most effective way to end a fight. Warily keeping an eye on Justin, she extended her other hand down to Shaw, who was still trying to extricate himself from his bicycle, and helped pull him to his feet. Justin turned abruptly and stomped off down the street.

"I'm fine, I'm fine," Shaw said to the multiple inquiries coming his way. "We've got some broken glass here, though. Sorry."

The manager bustled off to get a broom and a dustpan. The shoppers trickled into the store after him.

"Are you really okay?" Dorsey asked Shaw again. One of the patches of red on his shirt was a different and brighter shade.

"Crap," he said, clutching his right arm with his left. "I must have cut my arm on some of the glass when he pushed me down. Son of a bitch."

Dorsey examined the nasty-looking wound, which was bleeding copiously. "Shaw, I think you need some stitches there."

"No, no," he protested. "I've got a date. Come on, Dorse, it's not that bad. See?"

He moved his arm gingerly, which only caused the blood to start dripping on the sidewalk.

"Come on," she said, grabbing his good arm in a firm Big Sister grip and leading him toward her truck. "I'm taking you to Dr. Melba's."

"Wait!" he said. He pulled his arm out of her grip and reached for his wallet.

"What?"

"Can you at least please get me another bottle of wine? Please, Dorse?" His eyes were pleading.

As usual with Shaw, she gave in and was back in a few minutes with a new bottle of wine for him. She also retrieved his bicycle and put it in the back of her truck. He was in the passenger seat with his once-white dress shirt now wrapped around his forearm. He looked wan and vulnerable in his undershirt. He'd never been good around the sight of blood.

"Ready?" she asked him.

He nodded without speaking. Since it was now after six, she pointed the nose of the little truck toward Dr. Melba's house, not her office downtown. Dorsey insisted on accompanying him to the front step—she didn't want him to faint on the doormat as she drove away. Shaw, in turn, insisted on bringing his bottle of wine with him, saying she should go on home and get her groceries in the fridge, he was a grown man and could take care of himself, etc.

"Yeah, yeah, yeah," Dorsey said as they went up the front

walk. Shaw surprised her by peeling off to go around the side of the house.

"Kitchen," he said, gesturing with his injured arm. "I don't want to bleed all over her carpet."

He must have learned the layout of the house when he delivered the rocking chair, she surmised. He knocked on the wooden frame of the screen door with his good hand. They could hear low music playing inside the house and smell something good cooking. Pot roast, maybe.

"Shaw! What happened?"

Dr. Melba had flung open the door with all her usual vigor and seemed shocked by the sight of a bloody Shaw on her doorstep, although his scarlet stains were more Beaujolais than Type O.

"Well, come in, come in," the doctor told the both of them before Shaw could explain. After a three-second examination of his cut, she took him off to the bathroom to clean up. During the approximately ten minutes they were gone, Dorsey checked her watch and the clock on the wall about five times. Sarah was due to meet her at the house at seven and she hadn't even started cooking yet. She fidgeted while she waited, wandering around the kitchen and peering at Dr. Melba's possessions. She hadn't put much of a personal stamp on the house yet, but to be fair, she had been working hard on building up her practice in the six months she'd been in town.

Finally, the doctor and the patient returned to the kitchen. Shaw now sported a small bandage on his forearm and was wearing a clean T-shirt touting the Chicago marathon. Dorsey thought it was a bit above and beyond of Dr. Melba to loan Shaw a shirt, but maybe she was hoping to gain him as a permanent patient. In any event, he looked much better and had some color back in his cheeks.

"Well, thanks for waiting, Dorse," he said, "but I've got it from here. You can go home now. I'll settle up with Dr. Porter."

"Don't you want a ride?" she said.

"No, I'm cool. I can walk."

Dorsey guessed he didn't want her to drop him off at his date's house because he didn't want her to know who she was.

Probably a Lucchese, although Shaw usually had better judgment than that. Yuck.

"Don't you have raw chicken in the truck?" Shaw reminded her, clearly ready for her to be gone.

She did. And she was anxious to get home and start cooking. Not to mention she needed to change out of her work clothes herself.

"All right," she said, "then I guess I'll see you—whenever."

"Whenever," he said.

"Thank you, Dr. Porter," Dorsey said politely to the other woman.

"Oh, call me Melba," she replied, which surprised Dorsey a bit, but pleased her as well. Out of her white physician's coat and work attire, she seemed more relaxed in her home setting. She was casually dressed in sandals and a sundress, which made her look younger and less intimidating. Almost kind of cute, Dorsey thought. Well, almost.

"Okay, thanks, Melba. Have a good evening."

"You too, Dorsey."

She was only halfway through chicken Kiev when the front doorbell rang at seven o'clock exactly.

"Come on in!" she hollered. "I'm in the kitchen!"

She heard the front door open and close. Heard the clunk of Sarah's bag being dropped on a chair in the living room. Heard Sarah's distinctive, unhurried, heel-to-toe gait approach. She'd read about women getting weak in the knees but always figured that was romantic bullshit—what she was feeling as her lover drew near was far from weakness and most definitely not in the knees.

"Sorry," Dorsey called halfway over her shoulder. "I'm running a little late here and I've got my hands full of chicken breasts."

"I know exactly what you mean," Sarah murmured in her ear as she came up behind her, encircling her waist with her arms, then sliding her hands up to gently caress Dorsey's breasts. She kissed Dorsey's cheek, then the nape of her neck, rubbing up against her back.

"Not fair," Dorsey said, grinning. "Let me go so I can wash this goo off my hands and give you a proper greeting."

"There's a joke in there somewhere, I think, but I'll settle for a kiss," Sarah said, releasing her from the embrace. Dorsey washed and dried her hands at the sink, then pulled Sarah in for a long, slow kiss. And then another.

The kiss finally ended, but the moment lingered. Dorsey opened her eyes to find that Sarah's were still closed. She tightened her arms about her and touched her lips to Sarah's temple.

"Sorry about dinner not being ready," she said. "I got caught up at the store, then I had to help Shaw with something and I—"

"Hey, slow down, slow down, take a breath," Sarah said with mock alarm, sliding her hands down Dorsey's arms as she took two steps back. "We've got all night together. Right?"

Dorsey took her advice literally and breathed in deeply, then out.

"Right," she said with satisfaction. "All night. Goodman's in GC overnight and I'm not expecting Shaw home, either, so we've got the whole house to ourselves for at least twelve hours. And Mags and her mother aren't due back until Sunday afternoon, right?"

"Affirmative. So how can I help with this goo situation?"

Dorsey finished up the chicken while Sarah made a salad, then set the table in the dining room. They worked well together, Dorsey realized. There was no competition between them. They complemented each other, encouraged each other, razzed each other, had a hell of a good time together. It wasn't any one big thing—it was all the little things. She laughed more with Sarah than with anybody else—even Mags, she thought, with just the tiniest twinge of conscience.

It was odd, when she thought about it later, that it was cooking with Sarah—cooking, of all things!—that first made her realize she had fallen in love. This wasn't just a summer romance for her. It wasn't just sex with the Naked Silver Lake Goddess. It had grown into something much deeper and wider. Something so huge it almost scared her. Something she had always dreamed about, but never thought was meant for her. True love? She had no way of knowing, nothing to compare it to. But when she looked at Sarah, it filled her up inside. She didn't just want her physically. Something about being with Sarah made Dorsey feel like she was finally coming to life after a long hibernation. She loved touching Sarah, making love to her, exploring her body—but she also loved her patience, her kindness, her humor, her sense of adventure, her mischievous streak, her curiosity, her intelligence...

She put the chicken in the oven and set the timer, then got the fancy cloth napkins from her mother's china cabinet. Sarah was just finishing setting out the silverware and crystal goblets. Dorsey stood by her side and admired the beautiful table. It was all very domestic. Very...tranquil. As Sarah entwined her arm in hers, Dorsey felt like she'd known her all her life.

"Are we done?" she said. "What else can I do?"

"Hmmm," Dorsey replied, adding a napkin to each place setting. "Looks pretty perfect. Oh, wait, you can light the candles. Let me find some matches..."

"No problem," Sarah said, "I've got a lighter in my bag."

Surprised, Dorsey watched as Sarah returned from the living room with an ornate, heavy-looking silver cigarette lighter in her hand. She carefully lit both of the deep red tapers.

"Uh...do you smoke?" Dorsey asked her, hoping she'd hidden at least some of her disapproval of the habit. She'd never smelled any smoke on Sarah, though—surely she didn't smoke?

"Oh, no. I quit smoking a few years ago, thank goodness. This was my grandfather's lighter. He died when I was in college. It's just a keepsake now, although it does come in handy once in a while, like for candles. I can't quite bring myself to throw it out. It reminds of him, you know?"

"I know. I feel the same way about my dad's workshop, I guess. Hey, would you like to see it? We've got about forty-five minutes until the chicken's ready."

"Only if you show me the rest of the house as well."

Dorsey gave Sarah the full tour of the big old house in the waning daylight, saving the workshop for last. As they stood in the doorway, Sarah inhaled deeply, taking in the aromas Dorsey loved so much—the smell of the different woods, even the turpentine. She bent over the dining room table Dorsey was currently working on to look closely at the wood, then ran her hands over its shining, smooth surface. She looked up at Dorsey, who was standing there shyly awaiting her opinion, with something close to amazement.

"This is spectacular, Dorse. It's just so beautiful. And I can't wait to see what you're going to do with the chairs!"

"Well, thanks," was all a blushing, but delighted, Dorsey could manage to stutter in reply.

"No, I mean it," Sarah earnestly insisted. "Seriously, Dorse, you should be selling this stuff for thousands of dollars, not giving it away. I don't know if you know how talented you are."

"It's just a hobby..."

"Collecting stamps is a hobby, baby. This is art! I can see your heart, your soul in every piece of your work, Dorsey. I can see what it means to you. And it's beautiful—just like you are."

Dorsey looked at her for a long moment, her expression solemn, her eyes shining. But she didn't speak.

"Did you hear me?" an impassioned Sarah demanded, taking a step toward her.

"Yeah, but...did you just call me baby?"

What could have been another epic make-out session was cut short by the shrill buzzing of the kitchen timer, heard across the yard through the open kitchen window.

After dinner, they sat entwined together in the oversized recliner in the living room that was Goodman's prize possession. It was big enough so that even his extra large frame could stretch out in it and relax after a hard day at the store. It was more than big enough for the two of them. Sarah sat on Dorsey's lap with Dorsey's arm around her while they shared a bowl of ice cream and watched an old movie on cable, a favorite of both of theirs as it turned out: *The Deep* with Jacqueline Bisset, Robert Shaw, Nick Nolte and Lou Gossett, Jr. Okay, mostly with Jacqueline Bisset.

And when it was time, they went through the house together, turning off all the lights, then hand in hand, slowly down the stairs to bed.

CHAPTER ELEVEN

Saturday morning. Sarah was asleep in her arms. Dorsey relished the chance to watch her sleep. These moments with Sarah had become so precious to her. She carefully pushed a lock of coal-black hair away from Sarah's forehead, then ran a fingertip lightly over her delicate eyebrow, just to feel the smoothness of it under her finger.

She had almost forgotten what it was like to wake up with someone else. She could feel the warmth of Sarah's body next to hers under the covers. Could feel her breathing on her shoulder. She stretched lazily, trying not to wake Sarah.

Sarah stirred, then spoke without opening her eyes.

"Hey," she said sleepily. "Are you starving? I'm starving."

"I'll be happy to make you some breakfast," Dorsey replied. "Whatever you want."

"Whatever I want," Sarah repeated drowsily, then turned to bury her face in Dorsey's neck.

Dorsey waited a few moments, then when Sarah's breathing became slow and measured again, she gently untangled herself and went upstairs. She was at the kitchen counter drinking a glass of orange juice when she heard Sarah coming up the basement stairs not too much later.

"Are your brothers here?" Sarah asked in a stage whisper from the doorway to the stairs. "Do we have to be quiet?"

"Nope, I know Good's not back from GC yet 'cause his truck's not in the driveway," she said with a glance out the kitchen window. "And if Shaw's here, he needs to be up anyhow. He's supposed to be at the store by seven thirty this morning to open."

"What about you? Are you working today?"

"Yeah, I'm due there at noon."

There was fresh coffee in the pot. The kitchen was bright and warm with sunshine slanting in from the east-facing windows. Sarah had reclaimed her festival tank top, temporarily at least. Since their sleepover had been planned, she'd brought a few things of her own, including the flannel pajama pants she now wore. Dorsey appreciated just how low those flannel PJs rode on Sarah's slender hips. Sarah poured them each a cup of coffee while Dorsey checked out the food situation.

"Looks like we've got some doughnuts here. Some melon too. What appears to be somebody's sub sandwich. And eggs and bacon, of course, if you want the full deal."

"The coffee's fine for now," Sarah said. "Do you mind if we check out the news? I'm curious to see what the weather forecast is. I was going to check it on my phone but I can't find it. Maybe I left it at home."

They went back to the recliner in the living room where Sarah sat on Dorsey's lap with Dorsey's arm around her while they drank their coffee. Dorsey tuned in the local news from a Grover City station just in time for the weather report. More storms were in their future, which was not surprising for that time of year. At least it wasn't tornado season yet. She hit the mute button as a commercial came on and set the remote down next to her thigh.

"Hey," Sarah said, as if suddenly remembering something, "I meant to ask you about your bed—did you build that yourself?"

"Of course," Dorsey said. "Why? Does it matter?"

"Well, it just—" Sarah started, then stopped.

"What?"

"It just makes it even more special," Sarah said slowly, looking deep within her coffee mug. She leaned over to set it on the end table without making eye contact.

"So...was it special?" Dorsey asked her.

Sarah met her eyes then. "Yeah," she said, nodding. "It was." She looked at Dorsey, studying her for a moment. "And for you?" she finally asked.

"The best I've ever had," Dorsey said simply.

Sarah smiled a huge smile and leaned over to brush her lips against Dorsey's. "I'm so glad I found you again," she said.

Dorsey felt a burst of pure happiness. It just felt so right with Sarah—from the way their bodies fit together to the different ways they'd found to please each other already. It was like they had known each other in another life. Or for much longer in this one.

The kiss that followed was slow and tender and exploratory. Much was familiar after all the time they'd spent together in the week before, but there were still new surprises to be discovered. Dorsey's hips moved in the chair, a slight moan escaping her as Sarah teased her with short, sweet, wet kisses with a pause in between each that was only a moment, but on the brink of unbearably long nevertheless. She loved the feeling of Sarah's weight pinning her to the chair, holding her back while she strained ever forward, ever upward. It was then Sarah's turn to moan as Dorsey's hand moved up her flannel-clad thigh and in between her legs to first gently, then demandingly stroke and coerce. A gasp broke from Sarah's lips as she twisted to receive the tantalizing touch of Dorsey's strong fingers. Dorsey's lips were on Sarah's throat now, with Sarah's arms wrapped around her with all her might.

"Dorsey," she whispered, her breath laboring. "Dorsey Larue..."

The screen door on the back door to the kitchen opened with

its usual squawk, then banged shut as someone came in the house. Heavy male footsteps crunched across the floor and stopped at the sink, apparently, as water gushing from the faucet was the next thing they heard. In those frenzied few seconds, they went from frozen in shock to a wild, but silent disentangling to a more or less decorous presentation of Sarah still perched on Dorsey's knee. But at least both were upright and clothed, if a bit flushed and short of breath. Sarah ran her hands through her hair, trying to smooth it back down to a semblance of normality.

A half second later, Shaw wandered into the living room with a carton of milk under his arm, a paper-wrapped sub sandwich in one hand and a bag of chips in the other. He was still wearing the Chicago marathon T-shirt and stained khakis from the night before. He plunked down on the couch, put his feet up on the coffee table and started unwrapping his breakfast of champions. Glancing first at the TV, then over at the two of them in the chair, he gave them a big smile and a nod, said, "Hey" by way of a greeting and then "So what're we watching?"

He was so obviously and completely oblivious to the fact that they had just been having A Moment that the two women had to crack up. When they realized the TV was now showing some sort of nature documentary on warthogs—courtesy of Dorsey's butt changing the channel on the remote—more hilarity ensued. Dorsey's eyes were wet with tears when she finally pulled herself together.

"Sarah," she said, "this is my younger brother, Shaw. I don't think you two were formally introduced at the store. Shaw, meet Sarah."

"Nice to meet you, Sarah," Shaw said composedly, despite the fact that both women were still fighting off the giggles. He clearly had no idea what they were laughing about, but being Shaw, was courteously humoring them. Dorsey could almost read the indulgent thought bubble above his head: "Girls."

"So, where have you been?" Dorsey said to her younger brother. "Out all night doing who knows what," she said as a joking aside to Sarah. His only answer was a big grin that was visible around the edges of his sandwich.

Sarah laughed out loud and said, "You too, huh?"

Dorsey was pleased to find that Sarah and her younger brother hit it off immediately. Of course, Shaw was pretty easygoing anyhow. Just about everybody liked Shaw, with Justin Argyle being a rare exception. And while she was crazy about Sarah, she realized she'd been worried—without consciously realizing it—that her brothers might think differently. It was important to her that Shaw and Good liked Sarah. And she'd never worried about their opinions of her love life before. But everything was different now with Sarah. Different in the best of ways.

"You need a haircut, Shaw," Sarah was telling him. She turned to Dorsey. "Did I tell you I know how to cut hair? I took a course at the community college one summer, just for fun."

"You are just full of unexpected talents," Dorsey told her with a smile.

Shaw stood up to examine his shaggy locks in the mirror over the mantel. He peered closely at his reflection, his nose almost touching the mirror.

"I guess I could use a trim," he said musingly.

Dorsey was surprised—Shaw was never one to take much notice of his appearance. Haircuts were something to be endured rather than planned. Which was much the same way she felt, come to think of it.

"Well, come on," Sarah said cajolingly. She jumped to her feet as well. "Let me cut your hair, Shaw. You won't regret it, I promise."

"I'm sure I wouldn't, Sarah, but I'll have to take a rain check, okay? I've got to get to work. Maybe Dorsey will let you take a try, though."

He headed upstairs to change.

"Hmmm, he's right—you need a haircut too, Dorse."

"Oh, I don't know," Dorsey said with some of her customary alarm at the thought of subjecting herself to someone else's idea of beautification. Although if she was ever going to subject herself to someone, it would certainly be Sarah...

"Come on," Sarah said coaxingly. "Please? For me? It'll be fun!"

"Okay," Dorsey said, caving but shaking her head at her feebleness. "For you."

They decided to set up in the kitchen as there was much more room and light in there than in any of the bathrooms. Shaw had left for work by the time Dorsey found herself in a kitchen chair, towel tucked around her neck and Sarah starting off with the electric clippers. Dorsey had jumped in the shower to quickly wash her hair before the cut—but then Sarah had jumped in too, which delayed the start of beauty school for another hour. She'd heard the phone ring while they were, ahem, shampooing but figured whoever it was would call back later. Both heads were damp as Sarah carefully buzzed the back and sides of Dorsey's head. She had redonned her PJ pants and the festival tank top to avoid getting hair on her other clothes. The buzz of the clippers at the nape of Dorsey's neck was always an unpleasant sensation for her. Unpleasantly visceral. Some sort of low-level, primitive response to a sensed, but unseen danger...

Sarah stood back and admired her work thus far. She had promised to just shape and trim Dorsey's existing buzz cut. Dorsey hoped she wouldn't regret this little exercise in trust too much.

"Not bad," Sarah said over the buzz of the clippers.

"What?" Dorsey said, craning her head around to look at her.

"I said—"

It was the screen on the front door they heard squawk then, its high-pitched shriek cutting through the monotone middle range buzz of the clippers. The front door wasn't locked. Who locked doors in Romeo Falls? Sarah and Dorsey exchanged a quick, questioning glance. Dorsey rose to her feet as Sarah shut off the clippers, the sudden silence somehow as startling as the interruption.

"Dorsey? You home?" The voice from the living room was unmistakably Maggie's.

Sarah shot Dorsey a horrified glance. She looked wildly about the kitchen as if she might bolt out the back door or down the basement stairs, but there was no time. Maggie's footsteps were approaching the kitchen doorway.

"Dorse? Goodman? Anybody? I'm looking for Sarah if you guys have seen her..."

Dorsey swallowed.

"We're in here, Mags," she called. What else could she do?

Maggie appeared in the doorway, a note clutched in her hand and a look of relief on her face.

"Oh, thank goodness," she began. "I've been looking all ov—"

Her voice faltered, then faded as she took in the scene. The two of them with their hair still wet from the shower. Sarah in her pajama pants, wearing Dorsey's tank top and clearly nothing else. Her expression was unreadable, her eyes dark as she looked away from Maggie's searching gaze.

After a long moment, Maggie said to her, "You didn't answer your phone." Her voice sounded odd. There was a flatness to it that was completely unlike Maggie's usual tones.

Sarah said, "I can't find it." Normal, everyday words, but they sounded off too.

Dorsey realized she was holding her breath and made herself breathe. There was a terrible feeling of pressure in the room, all the worse when compared to the happy time they had just been having.

Sarah was looking at Maggie now, something almost angry and defiant in her stance. Her chin was tilted upward recklessly. The shaft of late morning sun coming through the kitchen window put her cheekbones in relief and cast her eyes in shadow. Dorsey thought she'd never looked so beautiful. Sarah set the clippers down on the table with a jerky motion and walked carefully over to the basement door as if she weren't entirely sure her legs would carry her. She disappeared down the stairs without another word.

When Dorsey looked back at Maggie, she found that her lifelong friend was staring at her with something close to hostility. Oh, no, Mags, she thought despairingly—not you, Mags. Not you too.

"Why did you do it?" Maggie said to her.

"Why did I—what?" Dorsey replied in confusion. She and Mags had never fought, not once in their twenty years of friendship. She couldn't believe they were fighting now.

Maggie took two steps toward her, then stopped. "Why did you have to take advantage of her, Dorsey? You know she's fragile right now. Vulnerable."

Dorsey couldn't believe what she was hearing.

"Take advantage? Mags, it's not like that. You don't understand..."

"You're damn right I don't understand," Maggie fired back. She must have been incensed beyond reason to use the D word. "How could you do this to her, Dorsey? To me? Running around behind my back for Lord knows how long? Lying to me? You know this is wrong. You know she's not...like you."

"Look, Mags, I'm sorry you had to find out this way," Dorsey said in a desperate attempt to retrieve the situation. If only she could get Maggie to understand... "I know this is a shock, but maybe it's better for all of us that you know the truth. Sarah is gay, Maggie. And I'm...well, I'm falling in love with her."

Maggie's normally pink and friendly face was a shocking, angry white, with two red dots of color on her cheeks in startling contrast.

"She is not gay. My cousin is not gay," she said emphatically, raising her voice.

Dorsey felt her temper slip. She took a step forward and grabbed Maggie's arms, thinking perhaps the physical contact would break the awful spell. "What, it's fine for me to be all queer, but God forbid someone in your *family* is?"

Her voice was shaking. She looked down at Maggie and saw that she was crying. She released her hold and walked to the sink to stare blindly out the window. She could not believe this was happening.

"You are my family, Dorse," Maggie said in a voice choked with tears. A voice full of hurt. "You know that. But—"

"But what, Mags?" Dorsey turned around to face her friend.

"She is fragile, Dorse. I know she tries to act tough and all put together, but she's not been herself this summer. Losing her job and those pills and lying to me—that's not like Sarah."

Mags wasn't finished. "What I'm trying to tell you, Dorsey, is—is that you're not helping her. How can this possibly end well for either of you? As soon as she finds a new job, she'll be gone and you'll still be here. I don't know what you think you're doing with her, but—leave her alone, Dorsey. Just leave her alone. You're not helping her. Or yourself, in the long run."

There was a long moment of silence as the two friends stared at each other. The worst part was the ring of truth in Maggie's last statements.

But I can't help what I feel! Dorsey cried out inside.

The door to the basement stairs opened. Sarah stood there, dressed in her jeans and Henley shirt. She looked like she'd been crying too, but for the moment was dry-eyed and stony-faced.

"Let's go," she said to Maggie shortly.

"Sarah—" Dorsey began, but Sarah cut her off with a look that was both pleading and demanding, at the same time.

"I'll—" Sarah started, then stopped, seeming at a loss for words. "I'll talk to you later," she finally said.

Dorsey could see she was barely holding herself together. It was with an effort of will that she made herself nod and let Sarah go with Maggie, leaving her alone in the kitchen, with the dust motes doing their slow perpetual dance in the shaft of morning sun.

Her heart was breaking. Had she lost Sarah...and Maggie too?

CHAPTER TWELVE

The best week of Dorsey's life was followed by the worst. The days and nights seemed fragmented and disjointed. Broken splinters and shards. She moved in a nightmarish daze from home to work and back again. The pain of losing Sarah threatened to overwhelm her, but she tried her best to dull it with routine. She tried her best to hope.

She found out eventually that Maggie and her mother had come home early from the convention because Mrs. Bigelow's ankle had been bothering her. Maggie had been trying to reach Sarah on her cell phone to let her know they were coming back. When there was no answer and Sarah wasn't there when they got home Saturday morning, Maggie became alarmed and went out looking for her cousin.

Her cousin. Family. If only Sarah had been a complete

stranger, Dorsey thought in her bewildered agony. If only... If only there hadn't been Maggie in the middle of this. There had been a moment of hope when Maggie came to the store after a few days had passed. Just for a moment, she thought Maggie was coming to tell her everything was all right. That they were friends again. That she was okay with her and Sarah.

Maggie asked if they could speak in private, which was unusual in and of itself. Shaw watched the cash register while the two of them went in the back. But Good was in the office, on the phone with a distributor, so they found themselves talking in the alley behind the store. A suitably wretched place, Dorsey thought later, with the sour smell of the Dumpster and dirty puddles of water shining too brightly in the late morning sun.

"I'm sorry, Dorse," Maggie began. But her voice had that strange flatness to it again.

"I'm sorry too, Mags," Dorsey replied. And she <u>was</u> sorry. Sorry that Maggie's feelings had been hurt and that she had lied to her friend. Or at least concealed the truth from her. But she wasn't sorry about Sarah. How could she be sorry about even one minute of that? She'd fallen in love with Sarah—something she'd begun to fear she would never be able to do. If she could only make Maggie understand the depth of her feelings, she surely wouldn't make her choose between the two of them—would she?

"Sarah and I have had a long talk," Maggie told her. Okay, Dorsey thought.

"And she spoke with her mother in Chicago as well," Maggie went on.

Dorsey didn't know for sure whether that was a good thing or a bad one, but she felt something icy start to wrap its fingers around her heart.

"We're meeting with the pastor this afternoon," Maggie said. She seemed to be having trouble making eye contact with her old friend. Dorsey found her own gaze drawn to one of the dirty puddles. An iridescent streak of oil made it look almost pretty.

"We?" she said to Mags.

"Sarah and Mother and me. This is a family matter now, Dorsey. You know we all want the best for Sarah."

Dorsey looked incredulously at Maggie. "You're going to pray the gay away? Are you kidding me, Maggie? You know that's not how it works. You know me better than that—"

"This isn't about you, Dorsey. It's about Sarah. And giving her a chance for a good life. She's been through a lot, Dorsey. She just needs a chance to get her head on straight."

Dorsey stared at her best friend in the world, with tears that wouldn't quite come stinging her eyes.

"Nice choice of words, Mags."

"You know what I mean."

"I don't. I don't know what you mean at all, Maggie. All I know is you're my friend. You've always been my friend and I love you. And I thought you would want me to be happy."

"You can't be happy with Sarah, Dorse." Maggie's voice was loud in the ugly little alley. Her words bounced off the brick walls and the Dumpster.

"Why not?" Dorsey flared back at her. "Because she's your cousin?"

"Because she's fragile right now. She's vulnerable. I told you all this before. She needs our help and support, not you mixing up her mind with all this—"

"All this what, Mags? Gayness?"

"Look, Dorsey, I'm trying to tell you she's confused right now. She's going through a hard time and maybe she's not making the best decisions these days."

"So I'm a 'bad decision'?" Dorsey demanded. "Is that what you want to call it? Is this really you talking, Mags, or is this your mother's voice I'm hearing?"

"I think you better leave my mother out of this," Maggie said coldly.

Dorsey knew she had crossed a line, although she thought she was right. Vivian Bigelow must have been overjoyed to finally see the rift develop between her daughter and Dorsey. She'd been trying to break them apart for more than twenty years.

"Okay, you're right, I'm sorry. But, Maggie," she said pleadingly, "please try to see this from my point of view for just a second. I mean, did you ever think maybe you're being a little bit selfish, Mags?"

"Selfish?" Maggie said, clearly astounded by the idea. "What do you mean? That I want to keep Sarah all to myself? That's crazy."

"Maybe you don't want to keep her all to yourself," Dorsey said.

Maggie started to nod her agreement, but Dorsey's next words stopped her cold. "Maybe you just want to keep her away from me."

"Dorsey, I—"

"Is that it, Mags? Tell the truth. You owe me that."

Maggie looked at the brick walls on either side of them, then up at the sky, then finally back at Dorsey. Just like Sarah in the kitchen, in that moment just before discovery, when she had frantically looked for an escape route. But there was nowhere to go, for either of them. The truth catches up with all of us in the end, Dorsey thought bitterly.

"Fine, Dorsey," Maggie finally said quietly. "If that's the way you want it."

"There's nothing about this the way I want it," Dorsey told her, her anger now edged with despair. "But I want you to tell me the truth."

"The truth..." Maggie started. She swallowed, then began again. "The truth is—no, I don't want you to be with Sarah. I, I can't stand the thought of the two of you together like that. I'm sorry, Dorsey, maybe I shouldn't have told you that, or maybe I should try to understand—but I can't! I don't. I just...don't. And I can't stand to think of her with you. Like that."

Maggie was crying now, but Dorsey's not-quite-tears had disappeared. Despite the sun shining overhead, she felt a chill inside. Like she'd never be warm again. She looked at Maggie, crying in the alley, rooting in her purse for a tissue. She didn't look like the Maggie who had been her friend for all those years. She didn't look like someone Dorsey knew at all. Dorsey felt an ice-cold rage building deep in her gut. Without another word, she turned and strode back into the building.

CHAPTER THIRTEEN

The only upside to all the drama, Dorsey thought, was that she channeled all her wrath and pent-up feelings into her work on the Bartholomews' deck. She finished it three days ahead of schedule, working odd hours and late into the night, hammering, sanding and sawing by work lights clamped to the railings.

The last nail was driven after dusk on Saturday night. Dorsey swept the deck one more time, then loaded all her tools and materials into the back of her little pickup. She'd turned out all the lights but one, and left the bug-repelling mister going as the evening insects began to swarm. The night air was sweet, the sky starting to darken to that deep midnight blue she so loved. She sat on the steps of the deck, drinking a beer and watching the stars come out one by one.

She hadn't seen or heard from Sarah all week, nor Maggie

either, since that fiasco in the alley. Which was fine, since she didn't think she could stand to see Maggie right now. She wondered what she would have said if Maggie had *asked* her to stop seeing Sarah, instead of more or less forbidding her. Would she have granted her best friend that favor? Sacrificed what was probably just a summer fling for the long-term good of her friendship?

No. She wouldn't have. Couldn't have. Sarah had come to mean too much to her to just let it go. How many chances at real love does a person get in her lifetime? One? Two? Zero for a lot of people, Dorsey thought. She knew what she felt for Sarah was love. Knew she had to take her chance—maybe her one and only chance—at making it work.

She was so damn angry with Maggie she felt sick, like she was coming down with the flu or something. The nights were the worst, when she lay awake wrestling with impossible questions. How could Maggie turn on her like that, after twenty years of playing the dutiful and supportive friend? Had it all been just a lie? How could she expect Dorsey and Sarah to deny who they were? And who the hell had made Maggie queen to tell Dorsey to stay away from Sarah? What business was it of hers?

And yet...a part of her wanted to be fair, to give Mags a chance, to try and see it from her point of view. That objective part of her could see what a shock Maggie had endured. Dorsey knew she wasn't the only one who'd had her whole world turned upside down. As furious as she was with her best friend, she still thought Mags was a good person.

But that didn't make it right. In fact, it kind of made it worse. Maggie was wrong about this. Terribly, disastrously, cruelly wrong. Dorsey knew that in her heart even as she grieved for their devastated friendship.

And there was no one to turn to. Sarah had let her go. Just like that. Had bowed to the pressures of her family. Maybe, Dorsey told herself, what I felt was love and what she felt was—convenience. Sarah had played with Dorsey's heart, gotten what she wanted and moved on when things got tough.

Dorsey looked up at the thousand stars twinkling above her, but her vision was blurred by tears. They say it's your heart that gets broken, she thought—but she felt like every fiber of her being had been trampled, snapped, cut to the bone. Her hand shook as she raised the bottle to her lips.

Headlights swept the house as a car turned off the highway onto the driveway. Dorsey dully wondered who it could be. Not Maggie, she hoped. She knew they would talk again—there was too much history between them and it was too small of a town for them not to talk again, but she wasn't ready yet. Was it one of her brothers? She stood up, but could not identify the vehicle in the near darkness. Not until it pulled up behind her truck and parked could she make out the distinctive shape of the VW Bug. The driver's door opened, then closed.

"Hello, Dorsey," Sarah said from the foot of the steps. She looked tired and solemn. But beautiful.

Dorsey stood stock-still on the deck, her heart pounding in her ears. She felt almost like she was in the presence of a wild animal, like she shouldn't make any sudden movements and frighten Sarah away. She looked carefully over Sarah's shoulder into the Bug to see if anyone else had come along for the ride. With relief she saw that it was empty. She searched Sarah's face for a clue as to why she had come.

"Can I come up?" Sarah said, gesturing toward the deck.

"Okay," Dorsey said. That was all she could manage.

They sat down on opposite sides of the picnic table.

"I snuck out," Sarah said, with a trace of the mischievous smile that had had Dorsey's heart (not to mention other body parts) doing backflips over the past month.

You're a grown woman! Dorsey wanted to shout at her. *You don't have to sneak anywhere.* But she said nothing. Could not make herself speak. The pain was too intense.

The lone light on the deck brought Sarah's cheekbones into high definition. Her black hair had never been in such stark contrast to the paleness of her skin. Her eyes, though, were in shadow. Dorsey wondered if her own thoughts were as well hidden.

Sarah tried again. "I'm sorry, Dorse," she said, unknowingly echoing Maggie. "They've practically had me on lockdown all week. Between Mags and Aunt Viv, and my mother on the phone nonstop, not to mention that moron of a pastor, I haven't had a moment to myself."

Dorsey didn't know whether to believe her. Although she certainly looked worn down and sad...harassed and in pain. Dorsey had seen the same look on her own face in the mirror a lot lately. Sarah seemed worried at her continued silence. Afraid, almost.

"I wanted to call...wanted to see you," she went on anxiously. "But it's been such a hellish mess at the house. They wouldn't leave me alone... I finally just snuck out tonight when Maggie was in the shower and Aunt Viv got a phone call. I tried to call you from the pay phone at the grocery store, but your brother said you were out here. I was worried I wouldn't be able to find it by myself in the dark, but I did..." Her voice trailed off uneasily. "Say something, Dorse, for God's sake, just say something," Sarah pleaded.

Dorsey could only think of one thing to say. "Why are you here, Sarah?"

"To explain, I guess. Try to explain. My family, Dorse—well, they mean as much to me as your family does to you."

"I would never let my family make me deny my very identity, Sarah," Dorsey said as gently as she could, trying to take away some of the sting of the words. "Or try to make me into something I'm not."

"I'm not denying it," Sarah said. "Not anymore. If nothing else, this awful mess has freed me from that."

"So, Maggie—"

"Maggie knows I'm gay now. As does Aunt Viv, although no doubt she'll go to her grave still trying to find me a husband." Sarah laughed shortly, without humor.

"So, then—" Dorsey felt a surge of hope.

But Sarah shook her head. "They're totally freaked," she said grimly. "But they're still my family. I can't change that no matter how much I sometimes want to. Aunt Viv's a lost cause, she's in complete denial that anyone in *her* family could ever be a homo." Again that humorless laugh.

"But Maggie?" Dorsey asked.

"Mags is too smart to not get it. She does get it. She knows now that I'm gay and always have been. But that's not the problem."

"Well, what the hell *is* it then?" Dorsey asked with frustration.

"It's you, Dorsey."

"Me?" She looked at Sarah in surprise. "What do you mean?"

"It's just too much for Maggie to handle. It's hard enough for her that I'm gay, that I'm not the perfect paragon she'd built up in her mind. It's not even that I'm gay, I think—it's that I'm not what she thought I was. She told me she always wanted to be just like me—and now here I am, the exact opposite of what any red-blooded Bigelow would apparently want to be. Something her mother has always told her is abhorrent, as you well know. It's a shock to her system. And, on top of that, here I am running around with her best friend. She feels like you lied to her, Dorsey. Like we both lied to her. And I guess we kind of did."

"But she'll come around, don't you think?"

"I don't know, Dorsey. I don't know if she can do that. She's hurt and overwhelmed and confused, all at once."

Well, so am I, Dorsey thought. But she didn't say it. She wanted to, but the words just wouldn't come. She'd built up such a wall her whole life, having to watch every word, every action, be so careful. But now, when she wanted to speak, wanted to pour her heart out to Sarah, her carefully crafted wall was suddenly her enemy. She could not break through.

Sarah looked away, off into the night, then said in a quiet voice, "She told me she can't stand the thought of the two of us being together. She asked me—well, told me, to tell the truth, to stay away from you."

"She told me the same thing."

They looked at each other across the table for a long moment.

"Maybe she just needs some time to process," Dorsey said earnestly, but not sure if she believed that herself. "Maybe if we just wait awhile, she'll be okay."

"How long?"

"I don't know, Sarah. What do you think?"

"I don't know either, Dorse. I don't know if she'll ever be okay with it. What I do know is how I feel about you. You know I care about you. And I want to be with you. But...are we both willing to wreck our relationships with Maggie on the chance this might be a long-term thing between us?"

Pain pierced Dorsey like a dagger when Sarah said those words.

"*Might* be a long-term thing?" she echoed haltingly.

Sarah spread her hands in a gesture of appeal. "Well, come on, Dorsey, would you seriously run away with me if I offered? Your whole life, your job, your family are in this town. Would you leave them all behind just for me?"

"Sarah, can't you see—" Dorsey began, painfully.

"Look, let's be reasonable, okay? I can't stay here. You know that. I have to find a job, for one thing. You've known from the start that I was only here temporarily. Right?"

Dorsey nodded, unwillingly.

"I've loved the time we spent together, Dorse. But what happens when I have to leave? And even if we could figure that out, how can we build something together if it means we both have to cut our ties to Maggie?"

She sounded sensible, reasonable, laying out the facts. But who cared about the facts when what they'd had felt so good? Had they brainwashed her in one week, Dorsey wondered wildly. Had she forgotten so soon what it was like when they were together? The laughter they'd shared, the looks between them that said more than words ever could. Those moments in the dark, when it was just the two of them, entwined in warmth, the feeling of skin on skin?

Or had she never cared at all?

Dorsey felt stunned, felt as if she were turning to stone. Expressing her emotions had never been her strong point anyway, had never worked out well for her. Better to keep it inside, where people couldn't see, couldn't judge, couldn't make fun of you and insult you and hurt you. Couldn't disappoint you over and over again... But she had to try one last time. She wondered if her one chance at happiness in life was slipping away right before her eyes.

"Sarah," she said imploringly, trying not to sound frantic, "can't we at least try? Maggie loves both of us. Maybe with a little time, she'll change her mind. I can't believe she would purposely stand in the way of our happiness..." She reached out and took the other woman's hand. "Please, Sarah," she said, one last time.

Sarah looked doubtful. "I know she loves us, Dorse—but she's Aunt Viv's daughter too. That's hard to overcome. Her whole life she's heard nothing but how evil and wrong gay people are, from her mother, from her church, from this whole damn town. I mean, I know she's your best friend, and I know she knows you're gay, but she's never really *seen* you be gay, you know what I mean?"

Dorsey did know. She'd thought about that before herself, long before Sarah ever arrived on the scene. She'd wondered how Maggie would react if she ever actually had a real girlfriend. Would Maggie have been supportive? Repulsed? Friendly? Jealous? Meaning jealous in a totally nonsexual way, of course, because Dorsey had never thought of Maggie as anything but a friend and Maggie was one hundred percent straight. But jealous, nonetheless, in that possessive way women sometimes have when it comes to their closest friends. The question had never been put to the test, because all of Dorsey's liaisons had been away at camp, at festival or otherwise out of the public eye. She'd never even introduced Maggie to any of the women she'd been involved with. None of her relationships had ever made it to that level.

"You're not leaving town yet, are you? Maybe if we give it a few weeks...or if the three of us could talk it out..."

"I'm trying to do what's best for all of us, Dorsey," Sarah said, holding Dorsey's hand tightly. Her voice cracked as she struggled to continue. "I think...I think we shouldn't see each other for a while. Let's give everyone some time to cool down and see how it goes, all right? You need to give me some time to sort it out with my family—please. I'll give you a call."

But she had said something like that before—and hadn't called her all week.

"I have to go now, Dorsey," Sarah said quietly, slipping her hand out of Dorsey's. "They'll be worried about me." She waited a moment and then when Dorsey didn't respond said, "Are you going to be okay?"

Dorsey shrugged or nodded, she wasn't quite sure which. She felt weak and confused, and unable to meet Sarah's gaze.

Sarah leaned over and kissed her cheek. "I'll call you," she whispered.

Did she really mean that? Or was it big-city-speak for "I won't call you, because you're not what I'm looking for and we're done."?

Dorsey watched the VW's taillights fade in the distance. She felt suddenly exhausted, desperately tired and aching in both mind and body.

The drive back to town seemed impossibly long and dreary. There was nothing and no one waiting for her there anyhow. She still had her key to the Bartholomews' house, but couldn't stand the thought of going inside. She would sleep on their deck that night, she decided, under the stars. She had an old blanket in the truck and there were cushions on the deck furniture. The Bartholomews would never know and her brothers wouldn't miss her.

CHAPTER FOURTEEN

The next few weeks passed in agonizing slow motion. Dorsey went to work, and walked and talked, but on the inside, she was dying. She had too much pride to just lock herself in her basement bedroom and turn out the lights, even if that was what part of her longed to do. What little strength she had, she put into keeping her mind a blank. She did her best to not think at all.

Sarah had said she would call, but Dorsey hadn't really believed her. And she hadn't called. Not yet, at least... And Dorsey was too proud to make the call herself. Again with the pride. Is that all I have left? she asked herself when she allowed herself to think at all, which wasn't often. It hurt too much to think.

As mad as she was at both Sarah and Maggie, she couldn't help but miss them, especially with no other friends to support her. It seemed so unfair that they still got to have each other, while she had lost both of them. She saw their cars on Main Street from time to time. She'd come face to face with Maggie at the grocery store one day. Maggie was coming out the door with a full cart as Dorsey turned the corner to go in. Both stopped and stared for a moment. Neither spoke. After a few more seconds, Dorsey turned on her heel and left. She made Shaw do the shopping after that.

She hadn't talked to her brothers about what had happened, but both seemed to know through that strange small-town osmosis that spreads the news, both good and bad. Both were walking on eggshells around her, but she was too numb with pain to care. She wondered if Sarah was as angry with her as she was with Sarah. It was all so unfair. So screwed up.

Her woodworking was suffering as well. The dining room table and chairs she'd been working on in the woodshop were gathering dust. She couldn't summon the concentration or the will to finish the project. None of it seemed to matter anymore. Not without Sarah.

She got through the grinding misery of the days and the hell of the nights somehow. She saw no end to the agony, but something in her told her she had to persevere. Had to keep going, no matter what.

She came home one Friday night to find Goodman at the kitchen table, a pile of account books and paperwork pushed to one side. He looked upset, which wasn't surprising if he'd been working on the books. A mostly empty six-pack of beer sat in front of him, which was surprising. Good wasn't much of a drinker. She quickly counted. Despite his size, if that was beer number four in his hand, he was probably drunk.

"Good?" she said tentatively. "You okay?"

He looked up and seemed to have a hard time focusing on her for a moment. He squinted. "Hey, Dorshey!" he cried.

Yep, he was drunk. She sat down at the table with him and grabbed one of the two remaining bottles. She felt like getting drunk herself, but she knew it would only make her feel worse. One beer, then off to bed, she told herself. And tomorrow would be another day. And then another and another and another...all of them without Sarah. The knowledge stabbed in her mind like a ragged sliver of glass.

"How's it going?" she asked her brother. Anything to take her mind off her broken heart.

"Ahhh, that fuckin' home center in Grover. Taking all our business. Bastards."

"Yeah," she agreed.

There wasn't much else to say about that. They both knew the home center was probably going to put Larue's Swingtime Hardware out of business sooner or later unless something big changed. And that didn't seem likely. Good had tried everything he could think of, but the bottom line was always the same— they were being undersold by the competition and losing more business every day because of it. They had hopes that the upcoming annual Downtown Merchants Moonlight Madness sale would provide a temporary boost to profits, but they both knew that was all it would be—temporary.

"Oh, what does it matter anyway?" Good groaned. "You're going to leave, Shaw's going to leave. I'll be stuck here in this damn town forever."

"You love this town, Good."

"Yeah," he grunted, assenting.

"Besides, I'm not going anywhere. And neither is Shaw, as far as I can tell."

"Why not?" Good asked her. "Why don't you just get the hell out of here? I mean, what do you do all those sit-ups for anyhow?"

Dorsey stared at him, not expecting this turn to the conversation and not exactly understanding his point. He went on, his words only a little slurred from the alcohol. Maybe he wasn't as drunk as she thought. She provisionally upgraded him to tipsy.

"There's too many goddamn small-minded people here, Dorsey. You know that better than I do. And you deserve to be happy, Dorse. They'll never let you be happy here. Never. They're too ignorant and brainwashed and hateful for that."

He slammed his empty bottle down on the table almost hard enough to break it and opened the last one, downing half of it in one gulp. She was shocked. And amazed. She had never known he saw the town that way—the same way she did. Not Goodman, the big ol' friendly bear, the football hero, the guy you could always count on when you needed a hand.

"But Good," she protested, "I can't just leave you and Shaw and the store. I mean, come on—what would you guys do without me?" She didn't mention the workshop, but she knew Good understood what it meant to her.

Good answered her seriously. "I love you, Dorse. You're my sister. I love having you here. You know that. But this is no kind of life for you. And—no offense—but I could always hire somebody to help at the store if either you or Shaw left. If you wanted to leave."

She stared at him in disbelief. She had never heard him talk like this before. She wasn't sure whether to be insulted or...or what. Maybe it was just the booze talking. He probably wouldn't even remember this in the morning, she thought.

Goodman had one last comment for her. "You should just be happy, Dorse...you deserve it," he said again. His head sank down on the table, his big arms encircling it. "Happy," she heard him mumble again.

It was funny. Sarah had told her the same thing, that she deserved to be happy. And maybe Good was right—maybe she should leave. She could totally see herself in some big city somewhere, starting a brand-new life. Even without Sarah, she could see herself doing that. Excitement started to bubble up within her as she pictured it. But...the woodshop. It always came back to that. She couldn't imagine her life without her woodshop. And she couldn't take it with her. She was so tired and so frustrated with her brain going around and around in circles and always ending up in the same place. Stuck. She hated feeling that way. Why couldn't she just resign herself to it and get over it? She was born in Romeo Falls, she'd probably die in Romeo Falls. Alone and miserable.

Goodman had drifted off to sleep. A noise like a giant bumblebee trapped in a tuba was now emanating from him. She pried the beer bottle from his hand and draped the chenille throw from the back of the living room sofa over his shoulders.

"Good night, Good," she said as she turned to go down the stairs to her room for another sleepless night.

CHAPTER FIFTEEN

The plan was finally complete. It had taken awhile, but the who, the what, the where and the when were now decided. The what to burn had been the hardest choice—so many possibilities. But then things got real clear. It was perfect. The moment would come later that night, when no one was watching. A spark, a flame...and then an inferno. Was it too risky to stick around and watch for a while? Pretending to be part of the inevitable crowd of onlookers would certainly be delicious. Faking the look of shocked concern would be a hoot. But then it would be time to finally disappear. To leave Romeo Falls forever. Leave all those bastards behind...

It was time.

Moonlight Madness was in full swing at eight thirty on Saturday night. Dorsey and Goodman had been up to their elbows in customers throughout the evening, even if most of the purchases had been small-ticket items. The crowd was starting to thin out, though, as most people made their way to the town square. A bluegrass band from Grover City was playing a concert there after the stores closed at nine o'clock. Food vendors and local community groups had set up stands and tables around the square, so a carnival atmosphere prevailed. Even the weather had cooperated—clear skies and a gorgeous moon lit up the night.

"Is there a reason I'm here and Shaw is not?" Dorsey asked Good during a brief lull in the fray. She stooped tiredly to straighten out the duct tape display a toddler had found irresistible with its multicolored rolls of tape. George and Ira had taken refuge from the throng on top of a tall cabinet at the end of aisle three. George was visibly irritated by this change in his routine, his tail whipping back and forth. Moonlight Madness had taken place the same weekend every year of his life, but every year he was pissed off, nonetheless.

"He asked and you didn't," Goodman told her. "So I let him off early. I think he's got another date with his new lady friend."

"Who is that, by the way?" Dorsey asked him, still curious even in the midst of her own romantic disaster.

"I don't know," Goodman said with a shrug, "but I think he's getting serious."

Dorsey had to wince at that. She'd been trying so hard to keep Sarah out of her thoughts. She hadn't had much success, but Good's words somehow brought her feelings right to the surface. As fresh and as painful as ever. When would she ever get past this? she wondered.

"Sorry, Dorse," Goodman said sympathetically. He could tell she was hurting. "Have you—heard anything from her?"

It was the first time he'd directly asked her about her breakup with Sarah.

"No," she said shortly.

"But you and Maggie are talking again, right?" he said hopefully.

"Nope," she again said shortly. She busied herself with the duct tape more than was truly necessary. This conversation was taking her to the brink of tears and that was a place she'd been too often recently.

"You should call Maggie," her brother said, not letting it go. Which was somewhat unusual for Goodman. He was the older brother, it was true, but he was usually pretty good about minding his own business.

Dorsey was saved from having to answer by the jangling of the bell on the front door of the hardware store as someone threw it violently open. They both looked to see who had come in. Officer Gargoyle stood in the doorway, in uniform and looking agitated. They could hear the bluegrass band warming up in the distance, and something else as well. A siren.

"Goodman! Dorsey!" Gargoyle yelled at them urgently. "Your house is on fire!"

Dorsey sprinted the five blocks to her house. Both her truck and Goodman's were blocked in the alley behind the store by another merchant's vehicle. The overflow crowds for Moonlight Madness meant that all the legal parking spaces, and most of the illegal ones too, were full that night as the entire town and much of the surrounding countryside converged on Romeo Falls for the festivities. Officer Gargoyle was on foot patrol in the square, but got the call on her radio from Luke to alert the Larues.

Dorsey and Goodman had gaped at each other for a frozen second after Gargoyle's proclamation. Fear lurched in Dorsey's stomach as she realized she didn't know where Shaw was—was he safe? Was he home?

"Shaw..." she said in a faltering voice as she looked over at Goodman.

"Go," he told her. "I'll lock up and be right behind you. Go, Dorsey—now!"

She ran out the door and down the street toward their house—

the home that had been in their family for three generations. The night sky was eerily lit up with red and orange in that direction. The town's only fire engine passed her as she reached the corner of Main and Scott, the street they lived on. Other people were running now too, drawn by the smoke and commotion. She passed at least one middle-aged volunteer fireman who was huffing and puffing as she raced down the sidewalk. A small group of people was already gathered in the street near their house and in the yard of the home next door. Neighbors. Luke, with his back turned to her. Some kids on their bikes.

And Shaw! He was talking to Luke, partially screened by the large frame of the police chief. They both saw her coming and put out their arms to stop her as if she might run right on past them and straight into the blaze.

"Shaw," she gasped, skidding to a halt and grabbing one of his arms and one of Luke's as well. She bent over, about ready to pass out from lack of oxygen.

"Dorsey! Where's Good?"

Too out of breath to speak, she somehow mimed to the two of them that Goodman was on his way. With her breath returning and her mind vastly relieved to find her younger brother alive and unharmed, Dorsey turned her attention to the house. Which actually did not appear to be on fire upon closer inspection. Thick black smoke was rolling off the workshop, however, and flames were visibly dancing within. A window shattered as they watched. The firemen were pumping water on the blaze, but the small building was clearly fully engaged. The fire crackled and roared furiously, despite the efforts of the firefighters.

"Oh, no," Dorsey said in a voice not much above a whisper. "Oh, Shaw..."

Her brother put his arm around her shoulders and drew her close as they watched the destruction from the street. They both knew the workshop was full of combustible materials—not only the wood for Dorsey's projects, but turpentine, cans of paint, gasoline for the lawn mower... Dorsey knew she should be glad the house wasn't burning, but the loss of the workshop—on top of everything else—was almost more than she could bear. Her eyes filled with tears, but she couldn't let herself cry in front of all those people. Although why she should care about their opinions, she didn't know. A patrol car screeched to a halt behind the fire engine. Goodman and Officer Gargoyle jumped out and ran over to them.

Luke held out a handkerchief to Dorsey, which she gratefully accepted.

Seeing both his siblings there, Goodman said calmly, "You all right, Shaw?"

"Yeah, I'm okay."

"How...?"

"I was getting ready for my date," he told all of them. "I smelled smoke and looked out the back window. Looked like the flames were already six feet high, at least. I called 911, then came out here to hose down the back of the house and the roof."

"You may have saved the house, Shaw," Luke told him, clapping him on the back. "Good work, buddy."

Shaw shrugged and turned back to his sister. "I'm sorry, Dorse," he told her. "I couldn't save the workshop. I tried."

"Oh, Shaw," she said through her tears. She hugged him tightly, then let him go. "As long as you're safe, that's all I care about."

More people were gathering in the street as the word spread. It looked like half the town was there. People had migrated over from the square as this new excitement eclipsed the planned entertainment for the evening. Dorsey spotted Mariah Reinhardt and her teenage friends looking avid as they oohed and ahhed over the flames. The Sizzle Sisters were there too—they gave Dorsey sympathetic grimaces. Tanya Hartwell and Courtney Flugelmeyer were there, as was Justin Argyle, all three of them smoking, which seemed like a bizarre thing to do at a fire. There was a ripple in the crowd as someone forced his or her way through from the back. Dr. Melba popped out of the assemblage like a cork from a bottle and ran straight for Shaw, practically tackling him as she wrapped herself around him in a fierce embrace. It seemed incredible, but she appeared to be crying.

"Oh, Shaw, Shaw," she sobbed. "Thank God you're all right!"

Shaw looked a little embarrassed, but mostly pleased. He wrapped her in his arms, returning the embrace wholeheartedly.

Goodman and Dorsey exchanged a glance. Dr. Melba? *She* was the Mystery Woman? Well...why not? At least she could match him answer for answer on *Jeopardy*.

"My, uh, date," Shaw told them, rather unnecessarily, then turned his attention back to the new woman in his life.

Goodman was hailed by the volunteer fire chief, who was old man Gustafson's grandson Arlen. They walked over to the engine, talking.

Dorsey turned to find Luke right by her side.

"I'll wash this and return it to you later, okay?" she said to him, meaning the handkerchief.

"Don't worry about it," he said. They stood there for a moment, watching the firefighters hustle and yell, doing their best to put out the conflagration. As if to console her, Luke put his arm around her shoulder and casually walked the two of them a few more feet away from the onlookers. In a quiet voice, he said in her ear, "Shaw already told me there were plenty of accelerants in there."

Accelerants? Dorsey guessed that was the right word for the way the flames were racing up the sides of the workshop. The roof looked ready to collapse any second. The heat was scorching, even from nearly one hundred feet away. The cans of turpentine, paint and gasoline must have gone off like bombs in the intense flames.

Luke spoke in her ear again. "So what started the fire, Dorse?"

Startled, she pulled away from him to face him squarely. "I don't know, Luke! I haven't even been in there for a few days. Maybe...maybe a short in the wiring? I mean, you know none of us smoke. So what could have started it?"

"Does anybody else go in there?"

"No," she answered, not sure where he was going with this. "Who do you mean—like the cleaning lady? She doesn't go in there. I keep it locked anyhow when I'm not in there. What with the flammable stuff and the power tools in there, I wouldn't want any kids to get in, you know?"

She felt ill as she watched it burn. Her table, her chairs, all her wood and supplies, and most importantly, the tools...all gone. Just like that.

Luke put his arm around her shoulders again, which she didn't much care for, but she could tell he was up to something. He was clearly in detective mode. He again turned her so they were facing away from the crowd and spoke quietly, but distinctly, into her ear, giving the appearance of a consoling friend, but in reality, doing his job.

"It's too soon to say if it's arson, but—"

"*Arson*?" Dorsey was shocked. "In Romeo Falls? You've got to be kidding, Luke! And why would anyone want to burn down our workshop? It's got to be some kind of an accident, don't you think? Arson..." She couldn't believe what he was saying.

"There's been a lot of strange things happening in this town lately, Dorsey. You know that as well as I do."

She nodded as Luke continued. "The point is, Dorse, if the fire was set on purpose—well, sometimes arsonists like to watch their fires burn."

His arm tightened around her as she started to swivel her head around to check out the crowd.

"Easy, easy. Let's just casually turn around now and you take a look and see if you notice anybody in particular, okay?"

He released her and they slowly turned to walk back toward the street. Dorsey tried to look distraught, which wasn't all that hard, and let her gaze wander over the crowd, which had grown even during the brief time she was talking with Luke. They were all people she knew, people she'd grown up with. Some looked concerned, some were enjoying the spectacle, some were both, but everyone's expressions more or less matched their characters. Dorsey couldn't imagine that any of these people—people she'd known all her life—would purposely cause such senseless pain and destruction. Sure, some of them were jerks, but they were her jerks, so to speak. She shook her head at Luke. He'd been checking out the crowd as well.

"All right," he said to her. "Let's try it a different way. Do you see anybody you don't know?"

"No," she replied. "I don't know everyone by name—some

of them are from out in the country or from GC, but the faces all look familiar. They've probably all come in the store at some point."

Luke tried again. When it came to his job, he was tenacious as hell. "Anything surprising or different or out of place to you? Anybody missing?"

Dorsey took another look as Goodman came up to her side, his consultation with the fire chief complete. They saw Maggie push her way to the front of the crowd, looking frantic, with Mrs. Bigelow slowly limping up behind her, her progress further hampered by her need to stop and gossip with just about everyone she saw. Maggie spotted her standing there with Luke and Goodman and made a beeline for them, looking mightily relieved.

Dorsey was still scanning the crowd. Luke watched her keenly, waiting patiently for her answer. The only one missing was...was...Sarah.

"Sarah!" Dorsey cried out desperately as Maggie ran up to her side. "Mags! Where's Sarah?"

"I don't know," Maggie told her breathlessly. "Thank God y'all are all right!"

In typical Mags fashion, she looked around for someone to hug, to share her joy and relief. Seeing that Dorsey was distracted, still searching the faces of the crowd for the one she missed the most—and sensing, perhaps, that she was not quite back on hugging terms with her oldest and best friend—Maggie settled for hugging Goodman, who looked surprised, but not displeased at the attention. He gently patted Maggie's back with one of his big paws while sharing a bemused look with Luke. Shaw wandered over to their patch of lawn, with Dr. Melba's hand firmly in his.

Dorsey stopped scanning the crowd and focused back on Maggie.

"Mags, where is Sarah?" she asked again. "Is she downtown?"

"I'm sorry, Dorse, I really don't know. She was supposed to come downtown with us for the concert, but she got a phone call at the house about an hour ago. Before I knew it, she'd thrown some stuff in her backpack and was taking off in her Bug. She wouldn't tell me what was going on—just said she'd call me tomorrow or the day after. Although we still can't find her cell phone—I don't know where it's gotten to..." Maggie added the last as an afterthought, her eyes getting big as she took in the full scale of the calamity raging in the Larue's backyard.

"Is she coming back?" Dorsey couldn't stop herself from asking.

"I don't know," Maggie said, shaking her head.

Luke said, "It could be important, Maggie. Do you have any idea where she went or when she's coming back?"

"I'm sorry, Luke, I just don't know. She took off so quickly, I hardly had time to say goodbye. But I'm sure she'll call."

Dorsey looked at Luke to gauge his reaction at the news that Sarah had taken off. Surely he didn't think she could be responsible for the fire? Surely...Dorsey looked again at the flames and thought of Sarah with her grandfather's silver lighter in her hand...and the look on her face when she had left Dorsey's house the Saturday before...and her words—so cool, so sensible, so fatal—the last time they had spoken at the Bartholomews' deck. Other words and phrases rang in her head: antidepressants... fragile...*strangers are trouble...nothing was happening before she got here...* She felt battered by her own confusion. Surely it was a coincidence that Sarah took off right before the fire started? Where had she gone in such a hurry? Without saying goodbye... Dorsey looked at the raging inferno that had once been her refuge and felt like she was going up in flames as well.

The volunteer firefighters had been gamely battling the blaze for close to half an hour. A major portion of the roof had fallen in, which was a good sign per a passing Arlen Gustafson—it helped to bring the fire under control. It was clear the firefighters now had the upper hand. A cheer went up from the crowd as the chief ordered first one, then another hose to be turned off. The steaming, smoking devastation that had once been a workshop looked like a mini war zone now. The firefighters continued to spray down hot spots and make sure the blaze didn't flare up again. Arlen had been poking around in the trampled, muddy grass around the workshop, going in wider and wider circles.

He stopped now, near the corner of the house, several yards from what had been the doorway to the workshop. He called Luke over for a quick conference, then Luke yelled for Officer Gargoyle who, at Luke's direction, had been dividing her time between crowd control and taking pictures of the scene with the department's digital camera. After a few words from her boss, she took some shots of whatever Arlen had found on the ground, then stood guard over it so no one would step on it.

Luke returned to the Larues. The crowd, which had started to break up when the fire was doused, seemed to re-coalesce as they sensed A Dramatic Development in the offing. Without the Gargoyle to keep them at bay, they were inching closer, forcing the people in the front to within a few feet of where Dorsey, her brothers and Maggie were standing.

"What did you find, Luke?" someone called out.

Keeping his voice down, Luke addressed his words to Dorsey, Goodman and Shaw.

"Looks like one of those wand-style firelighter things, half-melted from the heat. Being around the corner of the house there protected it from totally melting. Maybe somebody dropped it in a panic, running away—people sometimes do that when their fires take off quicker than they expected."

The three siblings looked at each other in dismay.

"You folks have one of those?" Luke asked.

"No," Goodman answered, his face grim. "Not that I know of."

"Shaw? Dorse?"

They both shook their heads. Dorsey added, "No, Luke. We've got matches, of course, but no lighter like that. Although we do sell them down at the store."

"Sold any lately?"

Dorsey and Shaw looked at each other. She could tell he remembered the transaction just like she did. She could hear the voice in her head: "What's up, La Puke?" The nasty voice of Justin Argyle. She could see him stuffing the change and his receipt in the pocket of his dirty denim jacket after he'd paid for the firelighter.

"What?" Luke and Goodman said the word simultaneously.

"Justin," Shaw told them.

All of them turned to look for the younger Argyle. He'd been near the front of the crowd all along and had been pushed to the very front when the crowd surged forward. He'd been trying to unobtrusively weasel his way back down to the street ever since he saw Arlen find the firelighter, but the densely packed crowd kept him pinned on the lawn. He then tried to slide down the front of the line to a point where he could escape, but Good was too quick for him. For a big man, he was nimble on his feet, as many a former defensive lineman in the county could attest. A few swift steps, then he reached out and grabbed the back collar of Justin's jacket, almost lifting the smaller man clean off his feet. It would have been an illegal "horse collar" tackle in a game, but no one was calling a penalty on Goodman in this situation. He unceremoniously dragged Justin, who was futilely clawing and kicking in an unsuccessful attempt to break free, back to the spot where Luke and the others waited.

"Easy there, Good," Luke told his old friend, but the twinkle in his eye was unmistakable. Goodman reluctantly let go of Justin, but made sure he was still within reach.

"What the hell do you think you're doing?" Justin angrily demanded, looking furiously around him at the people now encircling him. He looked hostile and irate, but pathetic as well. His hair was a sweaty mess, his face unshaven and his denim jacket as filthy as usual, with a gaping tear in the sleeve of the left forearm.

"What's this all about?" he snarled again. "If you think I set that fire, you're crazy."

It wasn't clear who his comments were directed to, but Dorsey noticed he looked everywhere but at his mother, still doing her duty by the corner of the house standing guard over the half-melted firelighter. Dorsey looked away quickly after catching a glimpse of her white, agonized face. She hadn't moved from her post, but was straining to see and hear what was going on with her only child.

Luke stared straight at Justin, who seemed unnerved by his silent, unblinking scrutiny. Luke looked at him without expression, but the contempt in his eyes spoke volumes.

After a tense moment in which no one spoke, Justin caved first and blustered, "Hey, man, you don't even know that firelighter's mine!"

Luke finally spoke. "What firelighter, Justin?"

There was a moment of silence as everyone realized the only way Justin could have known about the firelighter—which was out of sight on the ground at his mother's feet—was if he had seen it before. Justin's face was as white and twisted as his mother's as he began some angry retort. But Luke's words stopped him cold again.

"Fingerprints oughta settle it."

Everyone looked down at Justin's grimy, but ungloved hands. He jammed them in the pockets of his jacket as if he could hide his guilt that easily.

Shaw chimed in, "Doesn't look like you've washed that jacket recently, if ever, so I'm guessing the receipt is still in your pocket." His voice was carefully neutral, but Dorsey could see the gleam in his eyes. Seeing his tormentor finally get his due was sweet indeed. Shaw had turned the other cheek long enough.

Justin looked at him with hatred, looked at all of them with hatred, but saw no way out. There was nowhere to run. Luke pulled a pair of handcuffs from his belt.

Mrs. Gargoyle spoke for the first time. "Oh, no, Justin," she said softly. Despite her size, she looked strangely small in that moment.

Dorsey had never thought she would feel sorry for Mrs. Gargoyle, but standing there in the yard, with the smoldering ruins of the workshop and the twisted remains of her father's beloved tools which she'd never be able to replace, all she could feel was sorrow. For herself, for the workshop, for Gargoyle, and most of all, for Sarah and the love she knew she could never replace either. In the smoke and the darkness and the flashing multicolored lights from the emergency vehicles, she finally broke down and cried like a child as Maggie helped her into the house.

CHAPTER SIXTEEN

She ended up spending the night at the Bigelows. Goodman went back to the store, while Shaw said he would stay at the house, Dr. Melba still stalwartly by his side. Arlen had some of his firefighters stay too, to continue making sure no hot spots flared up overnight. The smell of the smoke and the knowledge of what had been destroyed was too much for Dorsey. She couldn't stay at the house, not that night. Maggie understood and took her home with her.

At first, it seemed like neither one knew what to say to the other. A good bottle of wine, which Maggie had hidden in her sock drawer, helped the conversation along. She retrieved it after her mother went to bed, a grumbling Carmichael in her wake. Dorsey and Maggie stayed up till the wee hours, talking and crying and talking some more in the kitchen.

After her second glass, Maggie said, "I was so shocked when I found out about you and Sarah, Dorse. It was all I could think about. I mean, at first, I *thought* I was thinking about the two of you, but eventually I realized all I could think about was *me*—how I felt about it, what my reaction was, what my feelings were. I know this doesn't mean much, if anything to you, but I prayed about it. A lot, Dorsey. And I spent a lot of hours talking with Pastor Reinhardt. I know Sarah thinks he's kind of a jackass, but he really helped me to see how selfish I was being. He's been through a lot with that Mariah, you know. He told me that being the father of a teenager has changed his perspective on a lot of things. Anyhow...what I'm trying to say is, I realized that Sarah is my family and if I love her—and you know how much I've adored her, ever since I was a kid—then I have to love who she really is, not who I want her to be. Especially not some juvenile, eight-year-old's vision of the perfect woman. I was being ridiculous holding her up to some imaginary standard I'd made up myself that had no relation to who she really is. I did some real soul-searching, Dorse, and at the end of that I realized: How can I say I love Sarah and then demand that she deny her very identity? It would be like me having to deny the things that make me who I am. I mean, what if I couldn't tell anyone I'm a teacher? I love being a teacher, you know that. I'm *proud* to be a teacher. I can't imagine having to keep that a secret that I could never tell anyone, not even my own mother."

"Or your best friend," Dorsey murmured, sipping her wine. It was a bottle of the white zinfandel Sarah so loved. Even with the fire, and Maggie's confession, and everything else, her mind still ached whenever she thought of Sarah, her Sarah. Where was she? Was she coming back? Would she ever see her again? Hold her again? Tell her that she loved her?

"Exactly!" Maggie said fervently. "When the pastor made me think in those terms, I finally started to realize, just a little bit, what Sarah's life has been like. What our family has made her life be like."

She looked at her lifelong friend with pain and understanding. "And a little bit what your life has been like too, maybe, Dorse. I'm so sorry. I was such a...such a...such an asshole!"

Dorsey had to smile at such strong language from Maggie, who hardly ever used such words. And certainly not in her mother's house.

"It's all right, Maggie."

"No, it's not! It's really not. I'm sorry, Dorsey—I feel like I completely screwed things up for you. No, let me finish. I need to say these things. I feel like I finally understand how lonely you must have been all these years, in this town."

Dorsey felt like she should be polite and demur, but then thought: Why? Why should I disagree? She's telling the truth.

"If I could never tell anyone I was a teacher, I'd have an awful hole in my life. Or, what if they wouldn't allow me to teach in Romeo Falls just because I was a woman...or just because I was *me*...I love this town, but I realize it can be a terrible place as well. I guess I finally figured out that the Romeo Falls I know and love is not the same town you grew up in."

They both thought about that for a moment. Dorsey couldn't help but think about Justin Argyle as well. He too was a product of this town.

"What I'm trying to say, Dorse, is if you and Sarah found even a little piece of love with each other, then I should be happy for you, not tearing you apart. I don't know if I'll ever forgive myself for the way I've acted. I'm so, so sorry, Dorse. I was stupid and wrong and I've done you an awful misdeed. You, my best friend. I'm so sorry, Dorse."

Dorsey reached over and embraced her bawling friend, patting her comfortingly on the back. She appreciated what Maggie was saying, but was also really hoping she was almost done. She'd had about all the drama she could handle for one twenty-four-hour period. But Maggie's confession and her emotions seemed to be escalating, not diminishing. A small part of Dorsey's brain wondered if Maggie was enjoying the dramatics, despite the painful subject matter.

"And the worst part is—" (there's a *worst* part? Dorsey thought) Mags was crying so hard now that Dorsey could hardly make out what she was saying. Whatever it was, it came out in almost a wail.

"What was that, Mags? I can't understand you."

"I (sniff) said...(sniff sniff) I said the worst part is... GOODMAN ASKED ME OUT!"

Yep, definitely a wail.

Dorsey sat perplexed. This was certainly a week for the record books. First, Shaw with Dr. Melba and now Goodman had finally stepped up and asked Maggie out.

"Well...did you say yes?" Dorsey asked her old friend.

Maggie had her head down on her arms on the tabletop, still crying and sniveling. She paused and opened one eye. She swiveled that eye upward, as if to check on Dorsey's expression before answering.

"...C-Can I?"

"Of course you can, Mags. If you want to, I mean. Hell, go for it, woman!"

"Really?"

"Really! For crying out loud, Mags... well, I guess you *are* crying out loud, so stop it will you and pull yourself together!"

"Okay," Maggie half-laughed, half-sobbed.

The two friends looked at each other in the yellow glow of the kitchen light. And realized there was some additional pale yellow light just starting to show at the windows. They had talked so long it was dawn. And just like the certainty of the sun coming up, they knew that bad things would sometimes happen. Sometimes they would hurt each other and let each other down. But the constant remained. Maggie and Dorsey, best friends forever.

They were hugging it out when Mrs. Bigelow came in with Carmichael at her heels. He growled at both of them in a nonpartisan fashion. A dirty little cast on his leg clacked on the linoleum floor as he walked. He and his mistress had matching limps. It wasn't funny—both Dorsey and Maggie knew that— but they struggled not to giggle. Dorsey controlled herself and started to say good morning to Mrs. B., but the older woman cut her off imperiously.

"Is that a WINE bottle on my table, Mary Margaret?" Mrs. Bigelow inquired of her daughter in a loud voice composed of equal parts shock, horror and extreme parental disapproval. Even Carmichael stopped growling and looked up at his mistress uncertainly. He decided to go hide under the table.

Dorsey looked over at Maggie, who had her eyes tightly shut, her hands gripping the edge of the table. She was looking rather pale. Dorsey wasn't sure if she was going to faint, scream, throw up or what. As she watched, Maggie opened her eyes, looked up at her mother and smiled sweetly. Maybe it was the wine. Maybe it was the lack of sleep. Maybe it was simply that Mary Margaret "Mags" Bigelow had finally had enough.

"Good morning, Mother," she said evenly. "I guess now is as good a time as any to tell you that I'm moving out next weekend. Pastor Reinhardt told me about a double-wide for rent down at the trailer park that one of the congregation owns. So you won't have to worry about me or the wine bottle much longer."

She stood up and put the bottle in the trashcan under the sink. Her mother gaped at her speechlessly, which Dorsey found to be a beautiful sight. Not to mention restful.

"And *you*," Maggie said forcefully to a bristling Carmichael, snapping her fingers and pointing with undeniable authority at the doggy door to the backyard, "OUT!"

The wayward beagle turned tail and slunk out the door without so much as a yip. Mrs. Bigelow too cast a wondering and hurt look at her only child, then flounced out of the kitchen in a whirl of matching polyester robe and fuzzy slippers. Maggie stood proudly by the sink, head up, shoulders back until her mother had completely disappeared down the hallway. If her bedroom door didn't slam, it certainly was closed very firmly.

Maggie turned to Dorsey, who was sitting there with her mouth half open.

"Holy cow, Mags," was all she could say.

"That's right," Maggie replied, still talking tough. "I'm moving out. And if she doesn't like it, well, that's just too bad. I mean, if I'm going to start dating again, I need a little privacy, right?"

That was TMI for Dorsey, although she recognized the truth of it and applauded her friend's decision. She nodded mutely. Various muffled thumps and bangs were now emanating from Mrs. B's bedroom down the hall.

"She's probably just getting dressed," Maggie said with a trace of nervousness in her tone. She glanced down the hallway. "You think?"

"Uh, I think now would be an excellent time to go get some breakfast at the Blue Duck, Mags."

They made it all the way out the door and into Maggie's car before bursting into laughter like a couple of eight-year-olds.

CHAPTER SEVENTEEN

But where was Sarah?

Three days went by with no word. Dorsey saw Maggie or spoke with her on the telephone every day, just like before. Before Sarah. And every day Maggie would tell her, "Sorry. I haven't heard from her yet." Although she had found Sarah's missing cell phone. Carmichael had had it under the couch—it was chewed and mangled beyond repair when she retrieved it.

"At least that kind of explains why she hasn't called," Maggie offered up tentatively.

"Come on, Mags, there are plenty of other phones in the world if she wanted to call," Dorsey said.

"I'm so sorry, Dorse," Maggie said again.

She kept apologizing. Dorsey really wished she would stop. "It's all right, Maggie," she finally told her. "Let's just move past it. It doesn't matter now. She's gone."

Maggie looked more woeful than ever after that, but she stopped the apologies.

Luke had come by the store on Monday to tell Goodman that Justin Argyle had given the police a full confession. Not only did he own up to setting the fire, he also admitted to all the other recent acts of vandalism and malice—the highway sign, the butchered carnations, the dismembered possum, the church marquee, all of it. Dorsey was there too, to hear the news. She stood next to Good behind the counter and absently stroked Ira as they talked. George stared unblinkingly down at them from his perch on top of aisle three.

"But why, Luke?" she asked him, bewildered. "Why did he do it?"

"Which one? The arson?" the police chief asked her.

"Well, yeah," she said. "Why single us out? Why do any of it? What the hell is wrong with him?"

Luke looked around to make sure it was just the three of them within earshot.

"He's a fucking punk, that's what's wrong with him," he said forcefully. "And a creep to boot. Some people don't need a reason for the things they do, Dorsey—they just take out their venom on whoever's nearest and least likely to strike back."

"I'll be happy to strike him," Goodman interjected. "Several times, in fact. Do you know how much insurance paperwork I've had to fill out already because of that little bastard?" He shook his head angrily. The near destruction of his home was bad enough, but add paperwork to that and it became a hanging offense in Good's book.

"He apparently had some grudge against Shaw worked up in his mind," Luke explained. "Something about you too, Dorsey— something about the two of you humiliating him at the grocery store."

"He's crazy," she said heatedly.

"Yep, probably," Luke agreed readily. "I'm sure his attorney will be looking into that angle."

"How's poor old Gargoyle doing with all this?" Goodman inquired.

"Not too good," Luke sighed. "I heard she's thinking about quitting, but I'm trying my best to talk her out of it."

The two Larues shared a look which featured two sets of raised eyebrows.

"What?" Luke demanded. "She's one of my best deputies, if you come right down to it."

"What?" he then said again, seeing their continued skepticism. "Do *you* want to mess with her?"

Both hurriedly shook their heads no.

"Well, then, there you have it," he said with satisfaction.

All in all, it had been a good week for Luke. The string of crimes was solved, the mayor was off his back and he'd heard the highway department was getting ready to fix the vandalized sign in another week or two. He hefted his gun belt into a more comfortable position, chucked Ira under the chin and bade the Larues farewell.

After he left, Goodman finally and belatedly got around to asking his sister if she would mind if he asked her best friend out. Dorsey truthfully told him she thought it was an excellent idea.

"And don't forget to ask her about the books," she added jokingly.

"Actually, that's kind of what started this," he admitted. "I've been talking to her whenever she came into the store lately about some inventory control ideas and she has a lot of good suggestions. Some good thoughts about ways to expand our customer base as well. She really knows that MBA stuff inside and out. Did she tell you about her Wi-Fi idea?"

"Yes. But you're not just asking her out for business advice, right?" Dorsey questioned.

"No, no," Goodman assured her with a smile. "I've asked out the woman, not the MBA. I *like* Maggie—you know that."

Dorsey felt like she knew less and less about romance every day, but she was happy for her brother nonetheless. Happy for both her brothers, despite the grinding despair she felt deepen with each passing hour. Where was Sarah? Why hadn't she called Maggie? Why hadn't she called Dorsey? Had she decided to just disappear and take the easy way out?

The easy way out...Dorsey could take that herself now, if she wanted to. She mourned the loss of the workshop, but in a weird way, it had set her free. There was nothing now to keep her in Romeo Falls. She could go anywhere, do anything. Take off at a moment's notice. But having achieved the liberty she had so desperately longed for, she found herself at a loss as to what to do with that freedom. It seemed meaningless now, without Sarah.

She hoped she would get over her one day. And had absolutely no idea how to go about that.

On Tuesday evening, she locked up the store at five, then drove home. Dr. Melba had phoned to say she might come by later to look at the finished "re-imagined" furniture Dorsey had stored in the basement. Her friend in Chicago with the design store had asked her for some more photos. Dorsey halfway suspected Shaw might have put Dr. Melba up to it—both of her brothers were concerned about her, she knew, and trying to help in their clumsy male fashion. She was grateful for their support, but mostly just so tired. After a day of pretending to smile at customers, she just wanted to be alone in her room and try her damnedest not to think of anything at all.

Seeing the bright red Bug parked in front of her house was a physical shock. She felt a searing pain in her chest, which scorched her lungs and caught at her breath. She slowed, then stopped her truck in the middle of the street. Sarah was not in the car and nowhere to be seen. Dorsey could see the little VW was packed to the gills with boxes and suitcases. What did it mean? Was this the final goodbye? Dorsey felt a sudden urge to floor it, to squeal the tires and pull away with a vengeance, anything to avoid the confrontation which was coming. After a moment, though, she turned the wheel and pulled into her driveway.

Somehow, she knew where Sarah would be. She found her in the back, kicking at the ashes, staring at the devastation with distress written all over her fine features. She watched Dorsey walk up to her without a word. She looked stricken and tired, Dorsey thought. Should she just say "hi" like nothing had happened? A hug was definitely out of the question. In the end, the words she chose were plain and straightforward.

"I see you're leaving again," she said to Sarah. She was

surprised at how level her voice sounded. She didn't even feel mad anymore. The searing pain in her chest had settled into a dull weight. She hoped this wasn't going to take too long.

"I'm so sorry, Dorsey."

Dorsey couldn't tell if Sarah meant the fire or her leaving without a word or something else altogether.

"Yeah, well...where've you been?"

"L.A."

"As in Los Angeles?"

"Yeah, an old friend offered me a job out there."

An icy stab of pain pierced Dorsey at the thought of Sarah being so far, far away. Without her.

"A friend?" she said though, hanging on to her composure by the slenderest of threads. "What's her name?"

"*His* name is Irving. He used to be my editor. He's fifty-seven years old and has been married to the same woman for thirty years. He's helping to start up a brand-new magazine in L.A. and he wants me to be one of their staff writers. He called me on Saturday and I had to jump on a plane and book out there to interview with his partners on Sunday night. I had a second interview on Monday and they offered me the job then. It's a pretty amazing opportunity, actually. I just got back a few hours ago. I have to pack up and drive out there so I can start work next Monday. Any other questions?"

Sarah seemed tense and somewhat taken aback, perhaps, by Dorsey's seemingly cool reception. Her "Any other questions?" had been terse almost to the point of rudeness. She took a step toward Dorsey, almost challengingly.

Dorsey felt a great tiredness rising in her, filling all her empty spaces to overflowing. It threatened to overwhelm her. She wanted to sit down, but there was nowhere to sit, of course, in the ashes and rubble. She summoned her remaining reserves of strength, determined to get through what was probably her last conversation with Sarah with at least some small amount of dignity.

"I do have a question, Sarah," she said quietly. "Just tell me one thing—why are you here?"

"Dorsey, listen to me," Sarah said. "I talked to Maggie—"

"Is this about Maggie?" Dorsey found herself taking a step closer as well. They were face to face now, the white lunar landscape of the barren ashy yard at their feet.

"This is about me and you," Sarah said, reaching out to her, but Dorsey found herself pulling back.

Sarah seemed perplexed by her reaction. "Look," she said, "I'm sorry I didn't call and talk to you. I should have. I know that. I *did* call one night, but you weren't there and your brother sounded kind of drunk, to tell the truth... And then it was such a madhouse in L.A. and I didn't want to call until I knew something for sure. And without my phone...it just seemed easier to wait until I got back and could talk to you in person."

She looked pleadingly at Dorsey, who still did not respond. Could not respond. Images of the different sides of Sarah she had known passed through her mind—the childhood cousin she was so jealous of, the Naked Silver Lake Goddess from the festival and finally, the one she thought of as The Real Sarah. Her Sarah. The thought that this last Sarah was there to say goodbye and leave her behind—again, and this time forever— was too painful. A lump in her throat blocked any words she might have said.

"Dorsey," Sarah tried one more time. "Look, what happened with you and me and Maggie was awful and hurtful. And just plain wrong. It never should have happened, but it did. I can't undo that. But I've talked with Maggie and she told me she talked with you. She's fine with it now, Dorse. Can't you see what this means?"

Sarah's eyes were ablaze, her pale face heightened with color as she pleaded her case.

"What *does* it mean, Sarah? To you?" Dorsey finally said, not sure she wanted to hear the answer. "You're the one who backed off—the one who left."

"I only backed off because of the Maggie thing—we had to work through that, right? All three of us?" Sarah said, clearly confused by Dorsey's response. "And I only left for a job interview. But I came back—for you," she added.

"For what?" Dorsey demanded. "To pack up your car and say goodbye?" The one thing she hadn't ever heard from Sarah, she realized, was commitment. Maybe it had been just a summer fling for her. Just a roll in the hay with one of the locals. Tears rose in Dorsey's eyes. The hurt was too much. If Sarah didn't care for her...and she couldn't have her workshop...she really didn't know how she was supposed to go on...

"Dorsey Lee Larue!" Sarah exclaimed with exasperation, grabbing Dorsey's hands in her own and pulling her close. "I'm trying to tell you I want you to come to L.A. with me."

"What?" Dorsey was shocked, not sure she had heard her right. She forced back a surge of excitement—she couldn't allow herself to hope...

"That's right," Sarah was saying, still clinging to her hands, squeezing them tightly. "I want you to come with me. To L.A. Right now, Dorse, this minute—let's just jump in the car and go and leave this town behind."

"Why?" Dorsey's single word rang out and hung in the air between them. She needed to hear the words from Sarah, had to hear the commitment before she could give in to what her heart, her brain, her whole being was clamoring to do.

"*Why*?" Sarah shot back as if the answer was so obvious. She saw the look in Dorsey's eyes and seemed to finally grasp what she needed. She groped for the words, stammered, stopped, then started again. "Because...Because I love you, damn it. That's why. I love you, Dorsey. We belong together."

We belong together. There they were, the words Dorsey had been waiting to hear. We *do* belong together, she thought. She had known it all along. She just needed to hear Sarah say it. Needed to hear her Sarah say it. The beginnings of a smile curved her lips. Sarah saw it. A matching smile curved her own lips.

"L.A.?" Dorsey managed to say skeptically, although her heart was jumping madly with joy.

"Yeah, L.A. Why not? You'll love it—the beach, the smog, the traffic..."

"Swimming pools, movie stars..."

"You got it." Sarah laughed out loud, then resumed in a more serious and persuasive tone. "Just think, Dorse, you could set up your re-imagined furniture business out there. You know, start small, with a website at first, then get a few pieces placed in shops and other businesses, get the word of mouth going and maybe open up your own store eventually."

"Whoa, hold on, Sarah," Dorsey said. "I mean, yeah, I love your enthusiasm, but how am I going to do any of that with no tools and no money?" She gestured at the remains of the workshop behind them.

"Well, you can start with the pieces you have down in the basement and at the hardware store, right? And then how about I buy you a circular saw or whatever and then you pay me back eventually by making me some furniture? Like, you know, a bed?" she said with her irresistibly devilish grin.

"Do you even know what a circular saw is?" Dorsey asked, although she couldn't help but grin too.

"You can tell me all about it on the drive to L.A.," Sarah told her, twining her arm in Dorsey's and turning her toward the house. "You can tell me your whole list, whatever you need: hammer, nails, wood..."

"There's really only one thing I need, Sarah," Dorsey said as they walked to the door.

"What's that?"

"You. I need you, Sarah. Because I love you too." Dorsey stopped walking and pulled Sarah in tight to look deeply in her eyes, which were dancing back up at her.

"Oh, well, you better kiss me then."

Their lips met as everything else went away for a while.

Shaw and Dr. Melba were walking in the kitchen door just as Dorsey bounded up the basement stairs, backpack over her shoulder and jacket in her hand. Startled, they dodged out of her way as she raced past, a huge grin on her face. Over her shoulder, she called back to Shaw, "I'm going to L.A. with Sarah! Tell Good I'll call you guys when we get there! I love you! Bye!"

"Bye!" her startled brother yelled back.

Sarah was waiting with the motor running. There was barely room in the crowded trunk for Dorsey's backpack. She moved a few things around to make space. There was something rolling around on the floor of the trunk which kept getting in the way. Dorsey grabbed for it and came up with a can of spray paint. A moment of doubt, of panic, gripped her but faded just as quickly. It wasn't red paint anyhow, it was a neon metallic lavender according to the label. Probably for one of Maggie's many craft projects, she thought, smiling at herself and her foolish fear. She crammed her backpack in and closed the trunk.

"All set?" Sarah said to her with a smile as she climbed in the passenger seat.

"All set," Dorsey agreed. "Did you already say goodbye to Mags and Mother Bigelow?"

"Of course," Sarah said as she put the little Bug into gear and pulled away from the curb. Dorsey felt a twinge of guilt at leaving without saying goodbye to Mags herself, but she'd make it up to her somehow. Maybe Mags could come visit them in L.A. before school started. And if anyone would understand after all they'd been through, it would be Maggie, she knew. And Goodman too. Those two were perfect for each other, she decided.

"In fact," Sarah continued, "I kind of said goodbye to the entire town."

There was that devilish grin again. Dorsey couldn't see Sarah's eyes behind her mirrored sunglasses. A tingle ran up her spine. Surely, she didn't mean...

"Uh, what exactly do you mean?" Dorsey asked her. They were just leaving the city limits. Dorsey craned her head around for one last look at her hometown. Her gaze was caught by the dark green highway sign, still defaced by red spray paint, but with some additional text now added in a quite vibrant metallic lavender shade. She glanced over at Sarah, who was grinning like a maniac. She slowed, then pulled the little VW over to the side of the road so Dorsey could get the full effect. "Population: 3,557" had been downsized to 3,556. Dorsey had to laugh at that.

"You were really so sure I'd say yes?" she said to Sarah with a smile.

"Well, I *hoped*," Sarah said, grinning back at her.

Shaking her head in mock disbelief, Dorsey looked back over

at the sign and saw that Sarah had done more than just alter the population. The sign still said ROMEO FAILS instead of FALLS. But Sarah had added a punch line:

ROMEO FAILS
BUT JULIET ROCKS!

Their laughter rose triumphantly to the blue midwestern sky as they headed due west into the sun.

Publications from
Bella Books, Inc.
Women. Books. Even Better Together.
P.O. Box 10543
Tallahassee, FL 32302
Phone: 800-729-4992
www.bellabooks.com

CALM BEFORE THE STORM by Peggy J. Herring. Colonel Marcel Robicheaux doesn't tell and so far no one official has asked, but the amorous pursuit by Jordan McGowen has her worried for both her career and her honor.
978-0-9677753-1-9

THE WILD ONE by Lyn Denison. Rachel Weston is busy keeping home and head together after the death of her husband. Her kids need her and what she doesn't need is the confusion that Quinn Farrelly creates in her body and heart.
978-0-9677753-4-0

LESSONS IN MURDER by Claire McNab. There's a corpse in the school with a neat hole in the head and a Black & Decker drill alongside. Which teacher should Inspector Carol Ashton suspect? Unfortunately, the alluring Sybil Quade is at the top of the list. First in this highly lauded series.
978-1-931513-65-4

WHEN AN ECHO RETURNS by Linda Kay Silva. The bayou where Echo Branson found her sanity has been swept clean by a hurricane—or at least they thought. Then an evil washed up by the storm comes looking for them all, one-by-one. Second in series.
978-1-59493-225-0

DEADLY INTERSECTIONS by Ann Roberts. Everyone is lying, including her own father and her girlfriend. Leaving matters to the professionals is supposed to be easier! Third in series with *PAID IN FULL* and *WHITE OFFERINGS*.
978-1-59493-224-3

SUBSTITUTE FOR LOVE by Karin Kallmaker. No substitutes, ever again! But then Holly's heart, body and soul are captured by Reyna... Reyna with no last name and a secret life that hides a terrible bargain, one written in family blood.
978-1-931513-62-3

MAKING UP FOR LOST TIME by Karin Kallmaker. Take one Next Home Network Star and add one Little White Lie to equal mayhem in little Mendocino and a recipe for sizzling romance. This lighthearted, steamy story is a feast for the senses in a kitchen that is way too hot.
978-1-931513-61-6

2ND FIDDLE by Kate Calloway. Cassidy James's first case left her with a broken heart. At least this new case is fighting the good fight, and she can throw all her passion and energy into it.
978-1-59493-200-7

HUNTING THE WITCH by Ellen Hart. The woman she loves — used to love — offers her help, and Jane Lawless finds it hard to say no. She needs TLC for recent injuries and who better than a doctor? But Julia's jittery demeanor awakens Jane's curiosity. And Jane has never been able to resist a mystery. #9 in series and Lammy-winner.
978-1-59493-206-9

FAÇADES by Alex Marcoux. Everything Anastasia ever wanted — she has it. Sidney is the woman who helped her get it. But keeping it will require a price — the unnamed passion that simmers between them.
978-1-59493-239-7

ELENA UNDONE by Nicole Conn. The risks. The passion. The devastating choices. The ultimate rewards. Nicole Conn rocked the lesbian cinema world with *Claire of the Moon* and has rocked it again with *Elena Undone*. This is the book that tells it all...
978-1-59493-254-0

WHISPERS IN THE WIND by Frankie J. Jones. It began as a camping trip, then a simple hike. Dixon Hayes and Elizabeth Colter uncover an intriguing cave on their hike, changing their world, perhaps irrevocably.
978-1-59493-037-9

WEDDING BELL BLUES by Julia Watts. She'll do anything to save what's left of her family. Anything. It didn't seem like a bad plan...at first. Hailed by readers as Lammy-winner Julia Watts' funniest novel.
978-1-59493-199-4

WILDFIRE by Lynn James. From the moment botanist Devon McKinney meets ranger Elaine Thomas the chemistry is undeniable. Sharing—and protecting—a mountain for the length of their short assignments leads to unexpected passion in this sizzling romance by newcomer Lynn James.
978-1-59493-191-8

LEAVING L.A. by Kate Christie. Eleanor Chapin is on the way to the rest of her life when Tessa Flanagan offers her a lucrative summer job caring for Tessa's daughter Laya. It's only temporary and everyone expects Eleanor to be leaving L.A...
978-1-59493-221-2

SOMETHING TO BELIEVE by Robbi McCoy. When Lauren and Cassie meet on a once-in-a-lifetime river journey through China their feelings are innocent...at first. Ten years later, nothing—and everything—has changed. From Golden Crown winner Robbi McCoy.
978-1-59493-214-4

DEVIL'S ROCK by Gerri Hill. Deputy Andrea Sullivan and Agent Cameron Ross vow to bring a killer to justice. The killer has other plans. Gerri Hill pens another intriguing blend of mystery and romance in this page-turning thriller.
978-1-59493-218-2

SHADOW POINT by Amy Briant. Madison McPeake has just been not-quite fired, told her brother is dead and discovered she has to pick up a five-year old niece she's never met. After she makes it to Shadow Point it seems like someone—or something—doesn't want her to leave. Romance sizzles in this ghost story from Amy Briant.
978-1-59493-216-8

JUKEBOX by Gina Daggett. Debutantes in love. With each other. Two young women chafe at the constraints of parents and society with a friendship that could be more, if they can break free. Gina Daggett is best known as "Lipstick" of the columnist duo Lipstick & Dipstick.
978-1-59493-212-0

BLIND BET by Tracey Richardson. The stakes are high when Ellen Turcotte and Courtney Langford meet at the blackjack tables. Lady Luck has been smiling on Courtney but Ellen is a wild card she may not be able to handle.
978-1-59493-211-3